BOOKS BY EDWARD UPWARD

Journey to the Border (Hogarth Press, 1938)

...

THE SPIRAL ASCENT: A TRILOGY

In the Thirties (Heinemann, 1962; Penguin Books, 1969)

The Rotten Elements (Heinemann, 1969; Penguin Books, 1972)

No Home but the Struggle (Heinemann, 1977)

The Spiral Ascent was also published in one volume
by Heinemann in 1977, and reissued in three
paperback volumes by Quartet in 1978–79

...

The Railway Accident and Other Stories
(Heinemann, 1969; Penguin Modern Classics, 1972 and 1988)

The Night Walk and Other Stories (Heinemann, 1987)

...

Journey to the Border – a revised version (Enitharmon, 1994)
introduced by Stephen Spender

An Unmentionable Man (Enitharmon, 1994)
introduced by Frank Kermode

(with Christopher Isherwood)
The Mortmere Stories (Enitharmon, 1994)
introduced by Katherine Bucknell

Christopher Isherwood: Notes in Remembrance of a Friendship (Enitharmon, 1996)

The Scenic Railway (Enitharmon, 1997)

Remembering the Earlier Auden (Enitharmon, 1998)

The Coming Day & Other Stories (Enitharmon, 2000)

EDWARD UPWARD was born in 1903 at Romford, Essex, and educated at Repton and at Corpus Christi College, Cambridge, where he read English and History, and was awarded the Chancellor's Medal for English Verse. While at Cambridge he created with Christopher Isherwood a series of stories about the fictitious village of Mortmere. After graduating he became a schoolmaster; from 1931 until his retirement in 1961 he taught at Alleyn's School, Dulwich, where he was a housemaster and head of the English department.

Edward Upward's first novel, *Journey to the Border*, was originally published by Leonard and Virginia Woolf at the Hogarth Press in 1938. In the 1930s he also contributed stories to *New Country*, *New Writing* and the *Left Review* and was on the editorial board of *The Ploughshare*, journal of the Teachers' Anti-War Movement. For sixteen years he was a member of the Communist Party of Great Britain, but he left it in 1948 because he believed it was ceasing to be a Marxist party.

Between 1942 and 1961 Upward wrote nothing, mainly for political reasons, but in 1962 Heinemann published *In the Thirties*, the first part of his trilogy of novels *The Spiral Ascent*. The second part, *The Rotten Elements*, and the third, *No Home but the Struggle*, were published in 1969 and 1977. Edward Upward's other books include *The Railway Accident and Other Stories* (1969), *The Night Walk and Other Stories* (1987), and in this Enitharmon series, *The Mortmere Stories*, *An Unmentionable Man*, a revised version of *Journey to the Border* (all published in 1994), *The Scenic Railway* (1997), and the memoirs *Christopher Isherwood: Notes in Remembrance of a Friendship* (1996) and *Remembering the Earlier Auden* (1998).

OTHER ENITHARMON BOOKS
BY EDWARD UPWARD

Journey to the Border
introduced by Stephen Spender

An Unmentionable Man
introduced by Frank Kermode

(with Christopher Isherwood)
The Mortmere Stories
introduced by Katherine Bucknell
and with images by Graham Crowley

Christopher Isherwood:
Notes in Remembrance of a Friendship

The Scenic Railway

Remembering the Earlier Auden

EDWARD UPWARD

The Coming Day

and other stories

London
ENITHARMON PRESS
2000

First published in 2000 by the Enitharmon Press
36 St George's Avenue, London N7 0HD

Distributed in Europe by Littlehampton Book Services
through Signature Book Representation
2 Little Peter Street, Manchester M15 4PS

Distributed in the USA and Canada by Dufour Editions Inc.
PO Box 7, Chester Springs, PA 19425, USA

ISBN 1 900564 61 0 (paperback)
ISBN 1 900564 02 5 (cloth edition, limited to 50 copies, numbered and signed by Edward Upward and bound by The Fine Bindery)

British Library Cataloguing-in-Publication Data.
A catalogue record for this book is available from the British Library

The stories in this collection are previously unpublished.

Set in Bembo by Sutchinda Rangsi Thompson.
Printed in Great Britain by
The Cromwell Press, Wiltshire

Contents

THE COMING DAY

a novella

• 11 •

•••

THE SUSPECT

six short stories

• 73 •

The War Widow

• 75 •

Imaginative Men & Women

• 91 •

The Serial Dreamer

• 99 •

The Intangible Man

• 110 •

A Better Job

• 123 •

The Suspect

• 139 •

The Coming Day

a novella

THE STAFF of the Lindhurst Registered Care Residence, Cedric Durcombe thought, might or might not discover before daylight that he had walked out during the night. But he felt little doubt that when they did become aware of his absence they would assume he had gone back to his home – his own home, his own house, which they knew he had not wanted to leave. Two of his closest and kindest relatives, believing that he was no longer really capable of looking after himself properly alone there, had suggested that things would be much easier for him in the Lindhurst. Its reputation was excellent, they'd said, and they'd been to see the matron who had shown them a very pleasant room which would be available for him as soon as he was willing to have it.

Cedric told his relatives he was repelled by the idea of spending the remainder of his life in a Care Residence, but they reminded him of how he'd been complaining more and more about having to go shopping and having to cook his own food and wash up plates and wash his clothes in a washing-machine which constantly went wrong, in fact he had seemed to possess hardly anything that usually went right.

At last, reluctantly and unhopefully, he told his relatives that he would give the Lindhurst a try.

• • •

THE HOUSE he set out for when he absconded from the Lindhurst during the night was his own, he believed, but it was not the house he had been living in. It was very many miles away, far more than he could manage on foot.

Abandoning his pyjamas, he put on the underclothes and shirt that he had seen the Matron place in a drawer near his bed; and then, after quickly dressing himself in the suit he retrieved from a cupboard where he had seen her place it, he was happy to find notes for several hundred pounds still safely contained inside a zipped-up inner pocket of its jacket.

Putting on his short warm rainproof coat that could cover the upper half of his body and that came from the same cupboard, he passed along the quite brightly illuminated main passageway to arrive at the front door, which he discovered to have a lock he was unable to unlock. This might be intended, Cedric thought, to prevent sleepwalking residents from escaping out of the Lindhurst at night and dangerously trying to reach their own homes again. Fortunately he noticed a very small key hanging from a nail in the wall at least a yard away from the door, and taking this key he found he could use it to unlock the obstinate lock, and he became able to get out of the Lindhurst and soon to reach a gravelled path leading towards the main road.

•

Daylight had come when he reached the railway terminus just in time to catch a train to Brandsbrook, the town near which his second house was. He found that the compartment he hurriedly got into had only one other occupant, a youngish man with long blond hair who sat in a far corner seat. Cedric took the near corner seat diametrically opposite to his, not with any intention of distancing himself from him but solely because he almost fell into this seat in his hurry to enter the compartment. After a few minutes, however, a sudden feeling of alarm made Cedric decide to speak to the man, despite his now having begun busily writing in a notebook he held on his knees.

'Excuse me, but could you tell me if this train stops at Brandsbrook? I was in too much of a rush at the Terminus to look carefully at the train departures board.'

'Yes,' the man said pleasantly, 'it does. At least I hope it does. I have an appointment with a valuable customer there.'

Cedric couldn't immediately think of anything he could say to this, and also he wished to avoid interrupting the man's writing any further; but the man rapidly finished it, and after pocketing his notebook he soon showed an eagerness to tell Cedric something more about the work he did at Brandsbrook.

'By profession I am a quantity surveyor, a *qualified* quantity surveyor as I like to call myself.' He smiled. 'I began my working life as an actor, which is what I really wanted to be, till I found myself too often out of work. However, "A man must live", as a self-justifying rogue is said to have told a wealthy aristocrat, who haughtily retorted, "I don't see the necessity".'

Cedric laughed, although the story – in its original French version – was not new to him.

The quantity surveyor continued, 'At present I am employed by that well-known firm, Gamley & Tryst. It's they who are constructing the high-rise flats that are extending gradually farther and farther along the sea-front. What an abomination!'

'I'm sorry to hear it,' Cedric said.

'Does this mean you haven't seen any of it yet?'

'I haven't,' Cedric said. 'Years have gone by since I was last in Brandsbrook.'

'May I ask, without seeming over-inquisitive, what has brought you here today?'

'Certainly you may. I have come to see a small house half a mile from the town on the far side of the brook. I inherited it long ago, but for various reasons I did not then want to occupy it myself, and I put it into the hands of a local house agent, trusting him to rent it to a reliable tenant.'

'Wasn't that a little bit rash?' the quantity surveyor asked.

'Well, rash or not, I went on trusting him, and regularly each month he sent me a cheque in payment of the rent, even during the war.'

Their train, a remarkably fast one, began to slow down smoothly, and soon it came to a jerkless stop. Cedric thought he remembered that in his younger days train journeys to Brandsbrook, though not always joltless, had been more leisurely and more relaxing.

'Here we are,' the quantity surveyor said, with a suggestion of regret in his voice.

Cedric stumbled hastily out on to the platform, and for a short while he stood movelessly there, feeling completely lost – so much larger this Brandsbrook station appeared to be than the station he had formerly known.

His bewilderment was evidently noticed by the quantity surveyor, who now informed him: 'The number of visitors and holiday-makers here has increased enormously of recent years, and you may find the whole town changed almost beyond your recognition.' Suddenly the surveyor looked as if he'd had a happy inspiration, and he added, 'What would you say to my being your guide? I have time to spare before keeping my appointment with Messrs Gamley & Tryst, and I would love to see your small house beyond the brook.'

Cedric felt he could only answer, 'Thank you very much.'

'By the way,' the surveyor said, 'I ought to have told you my name. It is Leonard Furnival, though I am ordinarily called simply Leonard. You can call me Leonard if you like.'

Cedric, slightly embarrassed, made no reply to this invitation.

Leonard didn't seem offended, and Cedric had the relieving thought that he need not call Leonard anything more than 'you' when speaking to him directly.

But as they started walking into the town Leonard asked, 'Would you mind telling me *your* name?'

'It's Cedric Durcombe,' Cedric answered abruptly.

'Well, Cedric,' Leonard said, 'what is your first impression of this town now? Do you recognise any of the shops?'

'I'm already aware of the disappearance of several – for instance, the fishmonger who used to have live lobsters crawling among the dead fish on his slab, and the butcher on the corner who was always laughing, and Martin's the bookseller who sold serious books, but good old Bailey the draper is still here, and apparently there are more shops than ever selling antiques.'

'Yes,' Leonard said, 'that really is extraordinary, to the point of being mysterious. However, the loss of many good shops is not mysterious. It is due to the supermarket that has been built by Gamley & Tryst half a mile outside the town. And I have to confess with shame that for this too they've used me as their quantity surveyor.'

'Why don't you throw up a job you're ashamed of?' Cedric bluntly asked.

'You are right,' Leonard said. 'That's what I've been inwardly considering ever since we started talking together this morning. And now I have an intuition that somewhere on the other side of the brook not far from your small house I shall find the solution to my problem.'

'What sort of solution?' Cedric uneasily asked.

'A theatrical one. I shall build a small theatre there which I think

I'll call *The Little Theatre*. It will stage mainly non-philistine new plays of a kind likely to appeal to a number of the people living in the area beyond the brook. I'm confident it will attract talented young actors who are not yet well-known. Like my own son Luke who's just left school and keenly longs to be an actor.

'I hope the plays you call non-philistine won't be of the sort that intelligent working-class people would find unintelligible,' Cedric said, thinking he detected a trace of artistic, and of social, snobbery in Leonard's plans.

'I'm afraid, Cedric, you may be more than somewhat behind the times,' Leonard said mildly. 'Samuel Beckett's *Waiting for Godot*, for example, was well understood by working people. But let us go and look at your small house.'

Cedric was no surer where to find his house than Leonard was, and when he finally found it he was at first not sure he had found it. It was an almost unrecognisable ruin. Its outer walls, though not its windows or outer doors, were still there, but the tiles were all stripped from its rafters, half of which had been smashed through by a single toppled chimney stack. How had all this happened? Could vandals have done most of it?

Leonard sympathetically shrugged his shoulders when Cedric asked for his opinion, though he did remind Cedric that farther along the coast there had recently been a hurricane which had caused widespread severe destruction, and that not surprisingly the press in reporting this had ignored the comparatively unimportant ruining of his small house.

Cedric said, 'I agree that what happened to my house is comparatively not newsworthy but I think I'll try to find someone locally who can tell me exactly how it happened, while you can go off to look for a suitable site where your theatre could be built.'

'Yes, I'll do that,' Leonard said, unoffended by Cedric's rather curt dismissal of him, 'and we'll meet again later.'

As Cedric walked away he noticed that his garden which used to be so well kept had run completely wild.

•

Within a hundred yards or so of his house, Cedric came upon an old man sitting on a teak-wood seat which had the name of its public-spirited woman donor incised into the wood he was leaning back against.

'May I sit beside you?' Cedric asked.

'Of course,' the old man said, in a sharply distinct voice which surprised Cedric.

Cedric sat beside him, and for a moment wished that the seat had been more comfortable than he found it. But he quite forgot his physical discomfort as soon as the old man spoke again.

'I have been watching you. I think you hope I might be able to tell you something about that wrecked house you were looking at with such interest.'

'Yes, I would be glad to hear anything you can say about it.'

'I may not have much to tell you that you don't know already,' the old man said, 'but perhaps you've not heard that the owner has disappeared, and they say he had not insured the house.'

The word 'owner' startled Cedric. Wasn't he himself the owner of the house? A frightening doubt came upon him, and an urgent need to remember clearly the time when he had inherited the house.

He briefly said thank you and goodbye to the old man, and walked away from him.

•

He was with his mother. They had come by train to find him a tenant for this house left to him by Norma, his godmother, who had been one of his mother's most devoted friends for many years and who had taken a constant interest in him as he grew up. She called the house *Little Garner* and the only reason she gave for having chosen this name was that she liked the sound of it. But she had her secrets.

A local house agent was due to meet them at the house at four o'clock today, bringing with him a prospective tenant, Cedric's mother having arranged this by letter – though she knew nothing about the agent's reliability or honesty.

Cedric had recently received the keys of the house from Norma's solicitor by registered post, and he and his mother were early enough to be able to look over the rooms before the agent's arrival.

•

There was evidence in the main downstair room that Norma shared his mother's fondness for antique furniture. He saw an impressive dark oak bureau and a Sheraton table and armchairs. Also he saw a window seat that had cushions with Art Nouveau designs on their covers. But the room as a whole was almost over-full of smaller objects which had no doubt been specially treasured by Norma, among them two china dogs (one at each side of the fireplace), framed samplers attached to the walls, candle-lamps on the mantelpiece, and a long-handled toasting fork hanging from a hook below the mantelshelf.

'Where can the kitchen be?' Cedric asked, priding himself on having thought of this.

His mother pointed towards a closed jade green door and said, 'We'll try that.'

They did, and found themselves in an adequately-equipped kitchen containing a gas cooker, a kitchen cabinet well stocked with glasses, plates and tinned foods; and also there was a larder which had a sheet of wire gauze drawn across its window.

'That seems a bit old-fashioned, and not very hygienic,' Cedric commented.

'Yes,' his mother agreed. 'I can only think it must have been because she was still working hard as matron of that important hospital in the north when she was having this house built for her retirement, and the builder gave the larder a wire-meshed window without consulting her about it.'

Next they went upstairs and found three bedrooms, one of them presumably her own, and none of them containing a double bed. Evidently she did not contemplate having friends to stay with her who weren't single.

The only other rooms upstairs were a bathroom and a lavatory.

Cedric said, 'Does this mean that when she was downstairs and wanted –'

His mother interrupted him, 'Perhaps there is one downstairs that we have overlooked.'

•

There was a knock on the front door.

'That must be the agent and the prospective tenant,' Cedric said.

He and his mother hurried downstairs.

The agent had short-cut hair and a brisk manner. He introduced the prospective tenant to them as Miss Gibbens. She at once made a very favourable impression on Cedric. She had a pleasant face and voice and she seemed to take a keen liking to the house after being shown over it.

His mother explained to her that, though it had been left to Cedric, the furniture had been left to his sister, who, however, would not want to remove anything except the antique Sheraton table and armchairs.

'I hope you weren't looking for an entirely unfurnished house?'

'No, I wasn't,' Miss Gibbens said. Then after a pause she almost apologetically added, 'I haven't been told yet what the rent would be.'

The agent said to Cedric's mother, 'I think you hadn't quite decided on that when you wrote to me to arrange this meeting.'

'Yes,' she said, 'but since writing to you we have decided on a definite figure.'

She then told Miss Gibbens what this was.

'I am afraid it is more than I can afford,' Miss Gibbens said.

Cedric, greatly disappointed and without consulting his mother, said, 'I'll gladly reduce it to an amount which you could afford.'

Miss Gibbens turned to him with a smile which had more than a trace of resentment in it, and said, 'Of course I can't accept that.'

For some while after she had departed in the agent's car Cedric could not be certain that he understood why his offer had made her resentful.

The agent said to Cedric's mother before he drove off, 'As soon as I get another prospective tenant I will let you and your son know.'

Within a week he wrote and informed each of them that he'd found a tenant named Mr McLaughlin, who was ready to pay the full amount they required and had in fact paid a month's rent in advance.

And it was paid with unfailing regularity to Cedric even throughout the war when he was evacuated from London with the pupils of the school which he taught at.

It continued to be paid after the war when the school was back in London and he was too busy settling down there again to want to travel to Brandsbrook to see his house and meet for the first time its regularly paying tenant.

But Cedric's sister Ida did call at the house, and she found living there a retired policeman and his wife, not McLaughlin. What was more, she discovered that they were paying McLaughlin a higher rent than he was still paying Cedric.

Cedric was furious about this, and he travelled down to meet these tenants who'd had the house sub-let to them by McLaughlin. He told them to pay the rent direct to him in future, and it would be the amount that he himself was receiving from McLaughlin, not the higher amount that they had been paying. They were very grateful to him, and he took a liking to them.

As soon as McLaughlin heard of what Cedric had done, he wrote him a letter full of menace. God, he wrote, had always punished with death those who had crossed him. Cedric ignored it and ignored the various other viciously abusive letters he got from this man.

He didn't hear till months later what happened next at his Brandsbrook house; and Ida, after visiting an elderly relative of her husband not far from Brandsbrook, was once again the discoverer who told him about it. She wrote to let him know that she'd gone to make a friendly call on the policeman and his wife – and to see how they'd been treating the house – but the door was startlingly opened to her by McLaughlin, who gave her a suspicious look.

'I was expecting to find the retired policeman and his wife here,' she said. 'Perhaps you could let me know where I could find them.'

'I haven't the slightest idea,' he said, and shut the door in her face.

•

She wrote to her brother, reporting her encounter with McLaughlin. She wasn't able to investigate any further, she told him, because she had to get back to her children, who had been left by her in charge mainly of a governess, her husband being too busy as a doctor to see much of them until the evenings.

• • •

AT THE TIME when Cedric discovered that his Brandsbrook house was destroyed, his own children were grown up and had got themselves good jobs and were happily married, and his own wife, their mother, for whom he grieved deeply, had died. But he was still in good health and he was free to go where he chose, and he chose to return incognito to Brandsbrook. He would look for someone who could tell him the whole story of the happenings at his house before its destruction.

But where would he look? In a pub? Rarely since his undergraduate days at Cambridge had he been inside one, but he knew that some pubs were better than others. Possibly a pub which was also a hotel would be better and more likely to be frequented by a customer capable of describing to him coherently and knowledgeably what had happened.

He didn't have to walk far before coming to a Brandsbrook pub-hotel which was enigmatically named, THE CAVE OF ENDOR. He couldn't remember having seen it when he'd last been in Brandsbrook. He hesitated for a moment or two, then pushed his way in through its swing doors.

He found himself facing a not very brightly lit central bar, and more shadowily on either side of this he saw a number of nooks where drinkers were sitting at small tables. He approached the bar. A tall barman and a rather grimly handsome barmaid were standing behind it. He ordered half a pint of pale ale, and she not very promptly got it for him. She asked him to pay more for it than he'd expected, but wanting to avoid starting a quarrelsome argument he paid without question and he thanked her with a smile - which she didn't even faintly reciprocate.

As he left the bar the intriguing idea came to him that she might be a fanatical adherent of a new religion called Endor, and that she had decided that he as an old man would be likely to have fixed opinions and would not be worth trying to convert.

He made his way towards a nook where only one person was sitting, a darkhaired man, hatless, unlike Cedric who wore a cap.

'I hope I am not intruding on you here,' Cedric said to the hatless man.

'Of course not,' the man emphatically said.

'Good,' Cedric said. 'This pub seems such a strange place to me that I wouldn't have been much surprised if some of these nooks were reserved for private meditation.'

The man laughed. 'Why does it seem so strange?'

'Its name, for one thing, "The Cave of Endor". Isn't that Biblical?'

'I wouldn't know,' the man said.

This time Cedric laughed. 'You are not a bible-basher, then?'

'Far from it,' the man said.

'Just before I left the bar to come to your nook I suddenly wondered whether the proprietors of this pub might be fanatical adherents of a new religion called Endor.'

'That's an interesting idea,' the man said; though his tone seemed to suggest that he didn't consider it plausible enough to be really interesting.

Cedric decided to say nothing more to him about Endor.

'May I ask if you are a native of these parts?' he said.

'Yes, I was born in Brandsbrook. And I once ran a small hotel here which I called THE GORAN. My own name being Goran. The hotel was a success, chiefly because of the steadily increasing number of visitors who took their holidays in these parts. Eventually I sold it for quite a bit more than I paid for it, and my wife and I moved into a comfortable flat. But, within a year, she left me.'

This surprising personal revelation alerted Cedric to the possibility that Goran might want to talk now, perhaps at considerable length, about his marital troubles.

In the hope of preventing the possibility from becoming an actuality, Cedric quickly said, 'I don't suppose you would have heard of a small house called *Little Garner* that I once owned in these parts?'

To his relief, this worked. 'I remember it very well,' Goran said. 'It was the only house here that was hit by the storm which did so much worse damage elsewhere along the coast.'

'I would be glad if you could tell me anything about what happened at the house in the years before the storm.'

'I could,' Goran said, 'and so could several of my acquaintances.'

'Did you know McLaughlin?'

'Did we know him? I'll say we did – one of the slickest of shysters who ever got away with it.'

'I knew he sub-let the house to a retired policeman and his wife. Could you tell me what became of them?'

'I could. You won't have forgotten that when you, the owner, found that the rent you had been receiving from him was less than he had been charging them, you told them that in future they were to pay the lower rate, and pay it direct to yourself.'

'How do you know all this?'

'It's common knowledge. But you may not have heard about the resulting fate of the unlucky policeman and his wife.'

'No I haven't.'

'Would you like me to tell you?' Goran asked.

'I would, very much.'

'All right, but I fear that it could make you feel guilty.'

•

'Soon after the retired policeman had begun paying the rent directly to Cedric, he and his wife were aware one night of some person or perhaps animal moving around the house. The light from inside the house indistinctly revealed the prowling shape outside. The policeman went out to confront the shape, but it evaded him. The same thing happened again on the two next nights. Why didn't he report this to the Brandsbrook police? Was he possibly afraid that they would suspect him of suffering from senile delusions? (As a matter of fact he had for several weeks felt shakily unwell and had been to the doctor who had prescribed pills for him which gave him strange half-awake dreams.) His wife on the other hand, though scared by the prowler, continued to be in good health. And then one morning the mystery was solved. Both of them saw McLaughlin walk round the house; as he'd every right to do, though the rightfulness of his doing so at midnight might be questionable.

'Within a month of their first sighting of McLaughlin by daylight the retired policeman died from a sudden heart attack.

'At the time of the funeral, and for a short while afterwards, McLaughlin kept away from the house; and the widowed wife was alone there with her grief. She was alone too with her growing dread that one day when she left the house to buy provisions, as she must, McLaughlin would slip into it and keep her out. And this was what he in fact did.'

•

'The excluded widow was received a week or two later into a mental hospital, where she stayed for the brief remainder of her life.'

'And you are responsible for all this,' Goran said to Cedric.

'No and yes,' Cedric guiltily said. 'The estate agent I trusted to keep me in touch with what was going on at my house was directly to blame for neglecting to visit the house, but I was even more to blame for trusting him and lazily failing to visit it myself.'

'The truth is that you are little better than a murderer,' Goran said, not quite unseriously.

'Well, one thing these happenings have taught me is never again to own two houses and to rent out the second one.'

Then Cedric remembered McLaughlin's most outrageous trick of all. He had placed an advert in the *Daily Telegraph* putting Cedric's second house up for sale. Cedric heard about this from his house agent in a letter urging him to come to Brandsbrook and to meet the man who had been tricked into buying the house from McLaughlin and who now wanted Cedric to rent it to him.

For Cedric the journey from London was specially memorable because of a very painful swelling that was developing on one side of his nose. Just after the war a colleague named Lester, who was temporarily sharing digs with him, developed a carbuncle on the back of his neck, and Cedric at Lester's request squeezed pus from it day by day until finally he caused the core of it to pop explosively out into the lint he was using. However, Cedric had apparently become infected, and but for the then recent discovery and use of penicillin the swelling on the side of his nose might have become a carbuncle that could have killed him. He must now wait for an injection till he got back to London, and the pain he at present felt didn't predispose him to speak calmly to the house agent waiting in an expensive Jaguar car at the station and hoping to take him to meet the cheated man who wanted to be allowed to pay rent for the house.

•

'How can he have been such a fool,' Cedric asked, 'as to buy the house without demanding the deeds from McLaughlin? Or is he in some way an accomplice of McLaughlin's?'

'No, I'm sure he is honest,' the house agent said, sounding quite shocked.

'Well, honest or not he'll have to produce the money to buy the house from me or I shall take possession of it.'

•

And the man did produce the money, and Cedric was glad to have this and to be rid of the house for ever.

•

But he wondered how his mother would react when he told her what he had done. After all, she had been an old friend of Norma's and she might feel a sentimental regret that possession of the house had gone to a stranger. Luckily, however, she was pleased that he had profitably sold it. And she was delighted with the unexpected present he sent her – something which was called a 'Tea's Made', consisting of a clock that could be set at any desired time and when this was reached a mechanism would be triggered to boil water ready for making tea.

•

Cedric might have gone on with the story of the 'Tea's Made' and might have mentioned how all too soon the mechanism had broken down, though the clock had continued to keep accurate time, and how his mother had been unable to find anyone capable of repairing the thing - but Goran said, 'Have you noticed an increasing stuffiness in the air of this nook?'

'Well, I think I can detect it now you've called my attention to it,' Cedric said. 'In my experience pubs do usually smell, but here the smell has a peculiar stuffiness of a kind that might be caused by a recently swung censer filled with smokily burning incense.'

Goran laughed. 'Perhaps the Cave might really be the temple of some new fanatical religion,' he not altogether jokingly said, 'This pub is what's known as a "free house", that's to say it is not owned by one of the big brewers, and the proprietors can do more or less whatever they like with it. But in any case let us get out of it and go.'

'Go where?'

'We can decide that when we're in the open night air,' Goran said.

Cedric followed him over muddy ground towards a looming black motor vehicle parked at the edge of a wood and almost as large, though not as high, as a furniture remover's pantechnicon.

'This is my motor caravan,' Goran said. 'We could spend the night in it; unless you would prefer to look for a hotel – an ordinary non-fanatical one, of course.'

'No,' Cedric civilly said (hoping he would not come to regret it). 'I would much prefer to accept your kind offer.'

Goran approached the rear of the van and inserted a small key into a keyhole low down on the side of it. A door slid open, and simultaneously eight aluminium steps unfolded themselves to reach the ground at his feet.

'I'll climb first,' he said.

He did so, and Cedric was glad that Goran extended a hand to help him up.

•

At the top, when Cedric was with him just inside the caravan, Goran pressed a button which switched on the light of an overhead electric bulb, and then he pressed a second button which caused the aluminium steps to upfold themselves and the door to slide shut.

'Now we are secure,' he said, 'and near the front of the van there is a metal chute that can be instantly let down in an emergency.'

Cedric would have liked to ask whether he knew of any particular dangers that made such precautions advisable at present: but Goran – whose eagerness to show off the many amenities available inside the caravan became increasingly evident – then pointed to what looked like a fairly large wooden cupboard with a window in the upper half of it. He pressed another button, and a light came on behind the window, revealing that the glass was quite thick and had an uneven surface which was translucent but not transparent.

'I have been told it's called Flemish glass,' Goran said, 'and in the wooden backside of the cupboard a smaller window containing the same type of glass is hinged at the top and can be raised or lowered according to the varying requirements of ventilation and temperature.'

Cedric laughed, and Goran added: 'The cupboard door is vertically hinged and can be bolted from the inside.'

Cedric laughed again.

'I gather you have realised what the cupboard is for,' Goran said.

'I believe I have.'

'Then I hope you will be interested to know that beneath this van there is a box containing chemicals which deal effectively with the excretions that drop into it.'

'I am interested,' Cedric said. 'I want to know what happens to the excretions after they have been chemically dealt with.'

'They are voided on to land which they can benefit.'

'Like a sort of fertilising manure, I suppose.'

'Yes.'

'Isn't there a danger that the excretion-destroying chemicals might poison the ground?' Cedric asked.

'No,' Goran said curtly.

Cedric, ignoring the annoyance he detected in Goran's curtness, questioned him further: 'How do you manage for water in this van?'

'That's a good question, as the saying goes,' Goran said, recovering his good humour. 'There is a large water-containing tank near the front of the van.'

'And what happens when that water gives out?'

'I simply drive the van back to my flat and refill the tank through a hose attached to a tap in my kitchen,' Goran said. 'Now let me take you to the front of the van.'

He led Cedric along a short narrow passageway with a blanket-covered bunk on each side of it.

'Here's where we'll be sleeping tonight,' he said.

At the end of the passageway there was a gap partly occupied by what Cedric saw as an ordinary domestic gas cooker.

'I use calor gas for this,' Goran told him.

'And where do you keep your food?' Cedric asked.

'Mostly in floor-cupboards under the bunks.'

'I assume it is tinned,' Cedric said.

'You are right, but for part of the year I can keep myself well supplied with fresh vegetables, and fruit, from the countryside,' Goran said, 'and I don't have to steal them, nor do I have to pay the farmers as high a price for them as I'd have to pay if I bought them at a supermarket.'

Forward beyond and to the right of the cooker were three khaki-coloured metal steps that led up to a low khaki-coloured metal door. Goran mounted the steps and opening the door he turned and beckoned to Cedric.

'Come up into my cabin,' he said.

Cedric came up and found himself close to the driver's seat. Goran had just sat down at the wheel.

'You could have the seat beside me,' he said. 'It's not uncomfortable, and I think you would prefer it to sitting on your bunk inside the van while I drive along green country lanes.'

'Yes, I would certainly prefer it.'

'By the way,' Goran said, standing up, 'do you feel like having something to eat now?'

'Well, perhaps I do, if it isn't too much bother.'

'No bother at all.'

Goran, followed by Cedric, turned and descended the khaki-coloured metal steps of the cabin and then briskly went to pull out a floor-cupboard from under one of the bunks. Lifting its hinged lid he selected a large tin, and holding this up for Cedric to look at he asked, 'Do you fancy Heinz baked beans in tomato sauce?'

Cedric didn't fancy them, but not wanting to risk offending his host he said, 'I do.'

Goran opened the tin by means of a tin-opener affixed to the side of the floor-cupboard, and after heating its contents in a saucepan on the cooker he spooned out with a wooden spoon a sizeable bowlful of the beans which he handed, together with another wooden spoon, to Cedric.

'You don't have to stand up to eat them,' Goran said. 'Just sit your bottom down on that comfortable bunk beside you, as I'm going to sit mine on this other bunk here.'

Cedric silently obeyed, not quite sure that he liked Goran's jocular tone. Wasn't it a bit – well – *ageist*, a bit condescending?

Neither of them said anything during their meal of beans. Perhaps now Goran was regretting having spoken to Cedric in that way.

'Did you enjoy them?' he asked.

'Yes, I did,' Cedric sincerely said. (He hadn't realised how hungry he'd become.)

'Now for the washing up,' Goran said.

'May I do it?' Cedric offered.

'Certainly you may.'

'Where?'

'In a basin in the – what would you call it? You as a no doubt well educated and historically well-informed man must know that it has had different names in different times and among different social classes. When you were a schoolboy how did you refer to it?'

'As the bogs or the rears, I think; but in Shakespeare's day to judge by his play *King Lear* it was vulgarly named a Jakes. My parents, if I remember rightly, used the word lav or loo.'

'Probably not loo; that came later, I think, but you are certainly well informed, Cedric. In what class would you place someone who called it a toilet?'

'Oh, definitely lower middle class,' Cedric said with a grin.

'And in what class would you place yourself?'

'Middle middle, the class that could just about afford to send its sons to "Public" schools – and to universities if they were bright enough to win scholarships to go there. Its girls of course never got beyond "High" schools.'

'And what about the upper working class?' Goran asked.

'They could be better off - especially if they worked on oil rigs – than the middle middle class.'

'Which schools would they send their children to?'

'State schools, for their boys and for their girls too, leading to mixed "Comprehensive" schools from which a Sixth Form minority could get accepted by universities, and a smaller minority still could rise eventually into the upper upper middle class.'

'And what would the lower lower working class do?'

'They would cease to be working class and would become "lumpen proletarians" – as they were called by a world-famous German writer,' Cedric knowledgeably said. 'They were capable of all kinds of crime, and no doubt the Nazis found a use for them.'

'One thing seems certain,' Goran said, 'that neither Germany now, nor any other advanced country claiming to be democratic, is as thoroughly infested with class snobbery as the country we live in. But nature summons me rather urgently at this moment to what I won't call "the bathroom", as I would do if I were an American with a loo and bath in the same room – an arrangement that must be extremely inconvenient when someone is lying in the bath and someone else wants the loo –'

'Your standing here telling me all this doesn't appear to tally quite with your saying that nature summons you urgently,' Cedric pointed out.

'How right you are,' Goran admitted. 'I'll go at once.'

'And I'll follow as soon as you've finished.'

When they had both relieved themselves, Goran said, 'If we are to get some sleep tonight it is high time we retired to our bunks now.'

•

Towards morning Cedric had an appalling nightmare which made him shriek aloud, and his shriek wakened him and wakened Goran too.

'What's the matter?' Goran, quite shaken by it, asked.

'I'm sorry. I had a nightmare. I dreamed I was being drowned.'

'No need to apologise. Your shriek was as good as an alarm clock. The light of a fine morning is shining into the caravan through pinpoint holes in the curtains. Let us get up at once and cook ourselves a traditional British breakfast of bacon, fried bread, eggs, tomatoes, mushrooms, sausages –'

'Not sausages!' Cedric exclaimed.

'Why on earth not?'

'Only abattoir workers, and of course their employers, know what filth from the bloodied floor goes into sausages nowadays.'

'Bah!' Goran said contemptuously.

• • •

DURING THE DAY Cedric gradually remembered his nightmare in greater detail.

He had dreamed to begin with that he was an infant in arms being carried through a churchyard past many lichened and lopsided tombstones towards, and then through, the doorway of an ancient church. Inside the church a tall surpliced priest stood facing a large stone font. A bosomy woman handed him over to this priest, who cradled him firmly in bare arms from which the cuffs, elasticated and decorated with lace, had been thrust back to the elbow.

•

Then a group of younger men, also surpliced, who were standing along steps in front of the altar at the east end of the church, began to intone slowly and in unison an English version of the famous lines of Sophocles from Oedipus Coloneus:

Not to be born is past all prizing best.
Next best by far when we have seen the light
Is to go thither swiftly whence we came.

It was at this point that Cedric, realising he was about to be ceremonially drowned in the font by the priest, shrieked, and woke both Goran and himself.

•

Cedric described this dream to Goran while sitting beside him in the van and being driven to 'a mystery destination' – as Goran called it.

'What do you mean by that?' Cedric asked.

'You insulted my sausages by asserting they contained scrapings from a bloodied abattoir floor, so I am taking you to see for yourself what a real large-scale modern abattoir is like.'

Cedric said nothing.

'Doesn't your blood freeze at the prospect?' Goran asked vindictively.

Cedric remained silent.

'I seem to remember that you raised no objection against bacon as one of the ingredients of the typical British breakfast we would cook for ourselves in the caravan,' Goran said. 'It was only my suggestion of sausages that filled you with revulsion.'

Cedric still did not speak. A feeling of hatred for Goran arose in him. 'I'll have nothing more to do with the man after this,' he thought.

'Oddly enough,' Goran said, 'our simplest way of getting to the bacon factory is by a path through a churchyard.

To have refused to go with him now would have looked like cowardice, and would in fact have been cowardice, Cedric knew.

•

The ancient churchyard he followed Goran through had lopsided and lichened gravestones in it like the churchyard in his nightmare. Abruptly and commandingly Goran said, 'Stop here if you don't want to be killed.'

They had come to a road along which at brief intervals motor vehicles hurtled past.

Goran, after peering quickly to right and to left, gave the order, 'Now, at once', and they both got hurriedly across.

The entrance to the factory looked like the entrance to an expensive hotel. Goran led Cedric through automatically opening double doors into an impressively Persian-carpeted entrance hall at one side of which there was a wide mahogany desk, and attached to the front of this in an oblong gilt-edged picture frame was a white card with the word **RECEPTION** printed on it.

Behind the desk sat a good-looking young woman, well-dressed and elaborately coiffured, who paused from the typing she was busy with and asked Goran and Cedric in a not altogether convincingly upper middle class accent, 'What can I do for you two gentlemen?'

Goran lyingly said, 'My friend here, Mr Cedric Durcombe ('how the hell has he discovered my surname?' Cedric wondered) is very keen to be shown over the bacon factory.'

The receptionist picked up a phone from her desk and spoke a few words into it.

'You will soon be attended to,' she told them, and then resumed her typing.

While they waited, Cedric became increasingly conscious of a perfume he had only vaguely noticed before. It was not pleasant, and it was too strong to be coming from any scent the receptionist might have been dabbing herself with. Perhaps someone in authority here had introduced it to disguise an offensive odour originating from a source beyond the entrance hall, Cedric conjectured; its function, in a more imposing way, could be the same as that of the blue soaplike objects that are sometimes hooked over the rear side of lavatory pans.

A door opened at the back of the hall, and the imperfectly disguised odour was intensified as a middle-aged man appeared wearing a white coat without a single spot of blood on it. The receptionist respectfully stood up from her desk.

This man, presumably the boss, or manager, of the factory, turned to Goran and Cedric and asked, 'Are you Government-appointed Inspectors, by any chance?'

'No,' Goran said.

'I'll admit I would be somewhat surprised if you were,' White-Coat said. 'The Government has recently sacked two-thirds of its abattoir Inspectorate – for the sake of economy. But we have nothing to hide. Are you perhaps militant vegetarians?'

'Not at all,' Goran assured him. 'We're here simply because my friend Mr Cedric Durcombe feels he ought to see how a really modern bacon factory operates.'

'That can very easily be arranged,' White-Coat said to Cedric. 'And what about your friend? Will he be coming with you?'

'I think I'll wait here,' Goran said, giving the receptionist a meaningfully admiring look.

'Follow me,' White-Coat said to Cedric.

The intensified hate Cedric now felt for Goran had the effect of temporarily dulling his acute apprehensiveness about what he would be seeing in the factory. Soon, however, White-Coat opened a red baize door at the back of the hall, and after ushering Cedric through it he shut it behind them both so that a small compartment was formed between it and a closed green baize door in front of them; and the same sickly sweet perfume he'd been aware of in the entrance hall, though far stronger, rapidly and almost suffocatingly filled the compartment. Then, as White-Coat opened the green baize door, an unmistakable odour of pig totally overwhelmed the artificial perfume.

White-Coat introduced Cedric to a man wearing a green overall and a green cap, like a surgeon.

'Scarott, here is Mr Durcombe who enjoys eating bacon but feels he has a duty to see how it is produced.'

White-Coat then turned and went back through the green baize door, leaving Scarott alone with Cedric, who began to retch violently as the pig smell became yet more intense. Scarott was sympathetic: 'You'll get used to it,' he said, 'when you realise that the animals feel no pain at all. They are electrically stunned before their throats are cut. Ah, and look, you are about to see it actually happen.'

A side door was abruptly opened, and a chain was slung round one of the hind legs of an almost man-sized unconscious pig which was then mechanically hauled up with its head hanging downwards so that a ready slaughterer was able to slit its throat with a twisting knife till the blood gushed down into a metal grating on the slaughter-house floor. But Cedric, in spite of the sick disgust he felt – a disgust that ensured he would never have bacon for breakfast again – was sufficiently in command of himself to be able to ask what was done with the blood that poured through the grating.

'Black puddings are made from it,' Scarott said. 'Not to my taste, but there's a considerable demand for them from some people. And now would you like to see the next stage in our production of bacon?'

'I can't say I'd like to, though I know I ought to and must,' Cedric said.

Scarott, opening a door into a rather dark, spacious and high-ceilinged room, called out a name - 'Joe!'

A man wearing a white overall spattered with brownish-red stains – which Cedric afterwards guessed to have been caused by a mixture of blood and entrails – came forward to meet them.

'Joe,' Scarott said, 'let me introduce you to Mr Durcombe. He is not an inspector of any kind but simply a private do-gooder who wants to feel sure that no cruelty is inflicted on the pigs in this factory.'

Joe bowed his head very slightly and briefly to Cedric, who returned his bow.

'Well, I must leave you now,' Scarott said smilingly to Cedric. 'I've appreciated meeting you.'

• • •

CEDRIC COMPELLED himself to follow Joe into the room. He soon saw what was going on there. A number of workers in overalls similar to Joe's were splitting open carcases which were hung from a steel rail by hooks driven through their hooves; and the blunt upper ends of the hooks were loosely curved over the rail so that they could be shifted along it. With big knives the workers struck downwards into the carcases, causing the entrails to slop on to the ground below them. Cedric had time to wonder suspiciously what was done afterwards with the entrails. Then he noticed how white and hairless the carcases were before they were slashed open. They might perhaps have been expertly shaved by workers using boiling hot soapy liquid, Cedric imagined.

Suddenly and with extreme horror he saw that one of the carcases was not a pig's but a man's. 'MURDER!' he screamed, and he rushed to the far end of the room and kicked his way through a shut door there.

•

Outside in the open air he continued to scream, 'MURDER!', until all at once he found himself completely surrounded by living pigs.

Not large pigs like the slaughtered ones he had seen, but middle-sized pigs who showed very evident signs of sensing that they too were on their way to be slaughtered. They began to attack Cedric – as if to revenge themselves while they still could on at least one member of the treacherous human race – and they would have bitten him to death if their swineherd, with a stick which was also an electric prod, hadn't parted them from him.

•

'What business have you to be here?' he was hostilely asked by the swineherd, a short broad-bodied man strangely dressed in a smock like a farm labourer from an earlier century.

'I have just seen the body of a slaughtered human being which was hanging among the carcases of slaughtered pigs in the abattoir. I have an absolute right to let everyone know that a vile murder has been committed.'

•

In a changed tone, contemptuous rather than hostile, the swineherd said, 'Allow me to tell you – and I'll tell you because I've realised you're only a well-meaning fool – that unless you remove yourself immediately as fast as you possibly can from this place you will most certainly be slaughtered and hung up like the human being you have just seen.'

Cedric hesitated for an instant; then he ran – though not as fast as in his younger days he could have run – towards an uphill group of fir trees; and at last reaching these he fell flat among them and became unconscious.

•

He was woken by a young woman with a rucksack on her back and a knife in her hand.

'Don't kill me,' he abjectly begged her.

'You are a Watchman employed by the bacon factory to keep a look-out for spies, and you've fallen asleep while on duty,' she said. 'Isn't that so?'

'It isn't,' he vehemently insisted, 'I am an escaper who saw the white body of a slaughtered man hanging up beside the carcases of pigs in that factory. I shouted, 'MURDER', and soon afterwards I rushed out away from the factory and uphill towards these fir trees. I was hoping to find some unobvious hiding-place among the trees which would save me from being discovered and brought back to be slaughtered and hung up with the other carcases.'

'I believe you,' she said. 'And now I can reveal to you that I am in fact a spy, a self-employed investigative journalist spying on the activities of the powerful company owning this abattoir. If you'd been a Watchman for the company I would have had to kill you or else become yet another human carcase; though I'll admit that this small knife of mine wouldn't have been a very effective weapon. I normally use it only for chopping up vegetables.'

Cedric was still too distraught to smile, which she may have wished he would. However, he felt attracted towards her.

She went on to say, 'We oughtn't to linger talking here any longer. We need to get away as quickly, and also as inconspicuously, as possible. But you'll do no more running up hills. We must keep to the valleys, regardless of how wet their streams may make us. I know of a "safe house", owned by a friend of mine, that we can aim to reach.'

•

The few streams they came upon did not wet Cedric's, or the young woman's, shoes much, but he stepped carefully. After a while she slid her arm under his arm, thinking perhaps that the long walk and his horrifying experience before it might be causing him to feel a little weary.

'What is your name?' she asked him.

'Cedric,' he said.

'It sounds Anglo-Saxon,' she said.

'That's what my grandfather thought when he persuaded my parents to give it to me. He was a great enthusiast for all things Anglo-Saxon, and he hated the Norman influence on the English language. But unfortunately the name Cedric was a mistake for Cerdic, the first king of the West Saxons. It isn't Anglo-Saxon at all.'

She laughed.

'Never mind,' she said, 'it's a nice enough name, I think. But what about my own name, Zaniah? How do you react to that?'

'Well, it's not exactly common. I mean that not many women have it. In fact you're the only woman I've met who has it. I like it. But I do think that one's liking or disliking of any woman's name depends very much on one's feeling about the woman.'

'Cedric!' she exclaimed with grinning severity, 'I do believe that you are being slightly flirtatious.'

She saw that Cedric was embarrassed by this, and to make amends she smilingly added, 'But in suggesting that you are being flirtatious I am really the one who is doing the flirting.'

There was a silence between them. She broke it by saying, 'Your grandfather had you called Cedric, and mine had me called Zaniah – which is the name of a star in the constellation Virgo. My grandfather was an enthusiastic amateur astronomer.'

Cedric smiled. Then he remembered the danger that he and Zaniah were in flight from.

'Why does the abattoir company have to murder human beings?' he asked.

'Because they are cheaper,' she said. 'And they are quite easily obtained.'

'How can that be?'

'The Government has adopted a policy of getting harmless long-term mental patients released from hospital "into the community" arguing that this may lead, with the help of sympathetic members of the community, to an improvement in their health, and even in some cases enable them to fend entirely for themselves. Yet all too often these harmless released patients become the prey of scouts sent out by the Manager of the abattoir.'

'But how can this happen without the Government becoming aware of it?' Cedric asked.

'They are aware of it, but they could have a strong reason for choosing to turn a blind eye to what's happening: there can be little doubt that at least one millionaire shareholder in the company contributed very generously to the fund which helped them win the last election.'

'I did read hints of this in a Sunday newspaper, but I wondered whether it might be just a dirty-tricks rumour put about by the Opposition.'

'Weren't you perhaps being a bit naïve, Cedric?'

'Why do you say that?'

'I mean, weren't you perhaps underestimating the extent of the corruption we are up against now? Sleaze is not confined to numerous ordinary members of Parliament: a very well-founded rumour is going the rounds that at least two Cabinet members are major shareholders in this same company.'

'If that's true,' Cedric said, 'what about the Prime Minister himself?'

'Yes, what about him, and what about all the other susceptible companies he and his likes have their fingers in or up, and what about the arms sales and the mass murders and the starvation and the pollution of earth and air and sea that the Governments of the richer countries of the world have been guilty of?'

'I know, but in spite of all this I haven't lost hope that the paupers of the world will at last learn to combine against these criminals,' Cedric said.

'I agree with you. In the meantime, however, if we are to live to support the world's paupers against their exploiters at all,' Zaniah said, 'we shall need to make our way as soon and as quickly as we can to my "safe house". We have five or six miles still to go.'

• • •

AFTER THEY'D WALKED a mile or so together she slid her arm under his, as she had done once before. 'Tell me about yourself,' she said now. 'Tell me how you earned your living before you retired.'

'I was a schoolmaster,' Cedric said.

'That sounds rather old-fashioned,' she said.

'The Grammar school I taught at was rather old-fashioned,' he said.

She laughed.

'Did you like your job?' she asked.

'Not much, but I liked it better than I would have liked any other job that I knew of.'

'Were you a good schoolmaster?'

'I was neither very good nor very bad; I was just medium.'

'You sound pretty negative.'

'Perhaps I was too negative – until my retirement from schoolmastering helped me to become more positive. But now it's my turn to ask you some questions.'

'All right. I'll try not to evade any of them.'

'How do you earn your living?'

'You've guessed it,' she said. 'I don't earn my living. The small left-wing journals that publish an occasional investigative article from me can't afford to pay me enough to live on.'

'Where does the money come from that you do live on?'

'It doesn't come from a teacher's pension or an old age pension.' She smiled.

'Nor does mine entirely,' Cedric said. 'I inherited some when my father died.'

'So did I when my father died. Also he often gave me money before he died, though he was not interested in the cause that mattered more than anything else to me. He was very fond of me and I was very fond of him.'

'What about your mother?'

'I didn't much like her. She was a keen business woman and I think she despised him for being unpractical.'

'Are you yourself married?'

'No.' She seemed momentarily startled by this question. Then she said, 'Nor have I been divorced; but when I was a university student I had a boyfriend at the same university as myself. It took me only a few months to realise how incurably self-centred and conceited he was. I broke with him. By the way, were you ever married?'

'Oh yes, for many years, and very happily.'

'Were you in love with your wife?'

'I'm not sure what you mean by "in love". I certainly loved her.'

'I was in love with my father,' she said, 'and he was in love with me.'

Now it was Cedric's turn to be startled.

Zaniah, noticing this, explained calmly, 'Of course there wasn't ever anything incestuous about our relationship.'

Cedric left it at that. 'Tell me about this "safe house" of yours that we must get to.'

'It isn't mine, actually. It belongs to a friend who was my governess when I was a child. After I grew up, my father bought it as a parting present for her. It's a cottage in the country, and she loves the country.'

'What makes you think it can be called safe?'

'She's well known and liked by her neighbours in the village where the cottage is,' Zaniah said, 'and they are used to her having visits from her many friends and relatives. Our arrival won't seem special to them at all.'

'Our stay might have to be quite a long one, I suppose,' Cedric said. 'Wouldn't we be expected to pay her something for it?'

'Of course not,' Zaniah said. 'My father's will provided very generously for her. And in any case if we did want to insist on paying her at least something, how could you get the money to contribute your share?'

All of a sudden Cedric remembered that when he had absconded from the Lindhurst Registered Care Residence he had taken his jacket with him, and in a zipped-up inner pocket of this he had been happy to find banknotes for several hundred pounds. Now as he walked on with Zaniah he thrust his hand into his jacket, unzipped its inner pocket and took out several hundred pounds in notes. He showed them to Zaniah, who was astonished. And so was Cedric himself. He had quite forgotten that besides these notes, and a few coins he had pulled out of one of his trouser pockets to pay the smileless cheating barmaid at the Cave of Endor pub, every item of the clothing he wore had been rescued by him from the Lindhurst Care Residence before he absconded. But what a muddy state his shoes and trousers were now in! Zaniah's old governess might at first sight of him wonder, he thought, whether Zaniah had charitably brought a senile old-fashioned tramp along with her.

•

Just before they reached the cottage Zaniah said, 'I shall be introducing you to my old governess surnamelessly as Cedric. Because, as I now suddenly realise, I don't know your surname. So if the enemy were to torture me in order to get it I wouldn't be able to give it.'

'But why should they be so keen to know my surname?' Cedric asked.

'Because this would help them to find out as much as possible about you and your past. I assume that a serious charge of industrial spying could be brought against you in a court of law.'

Cedric felt alarm.

'Also, I want to introduce my governess to you as Dorothy, in case they pressured you to tell them her surname, which I shall not reveal to you.'

'But you, Zaniah, do know her surname, and if you revealed it under torture it might help the enemy to track down everyone she has sheltered.'

'Yes, and my great fear is that then I might not have the strength to prevent myself from telling them her surname. There have been heroes and heroines who have resisted their questioners to the death, but I wouldn't presume to imagine I could ever become as heroic as they were.'

'How is it that we have begun talking about dangers and heroisms just when we are about to enter your "safe house"?' Cedric asked.

'I have full confidence in the safety of my "safe house",' she said, 'but we've got to be realistic. We must be alert to the possibility that the enemy might try to make a surprise search of the cottage. We would need to be watchful enough to remove ourselves rapidly away from it as soon as we glimpsed them craftily stalking towards it.'

'Which would mean we'd be ignominiously leaving your unlucky friend to face their questioning,' Cedric said, 'and she'd have to admit we'd been staying with her – because we would certainly have left a few traces of ourselves behind us – but she would truthfully deny knowing where we'd gone to, and they wouldn't believe her and would torture her.'

'It's time you stopped trying to demoralise yourself with these pessimistic speculations,' Zaniah said.

'You started them,' Cedric said.

'Perhaps I did,' Zaniah admitted, 'but I hope that when you actually meet her, as you soon will now, you will begin to recover from your pessimism.'

• • •

AS THEY AT LAST reached the cottage they saw Dorothy before she saw them. She was in her garden, wearing gardener's gloves and weeding a flower-bed.

Cedric became immediately aware that Dorothy was a woman who could be of his own age. He had been supposing, for no reason, that she would be some years older.

They took to each other at once when Zaniah introduced them.

Then Dorothy said to both Cedric and Zaniah, 'Come in, come in. You seem to have been paddling through mud. Go upstairs and cleanse yourselves, while I get a nice warm meal ready for you. You will find bath towels on the heating rail in the shower-room.'

•

Cedric followed Zaniah up the stairs.

'You'll have your shower before me,' she ordered him when they reached the landing at the top. 'And as soon as you've showered yourself and towelled yourself dry you'll cover your nakedness with the thick green dressing-gown which you'll see hanging from a hook attached to the door. This is the only garment you'll need to wear when we go down for our meal with Dorothy.'

'And will you, Zaniah, also be wearing nothing except a dressing-gown?'

'Yes, and it will be a beautiful red one.'

'But what about the dirty clothes we had on us when we arrived? What's going to be done with those, including the banknotes zipped up in one of my jacket pockets?' Cedric agitatedly asked.

'You funny old man,' Zaniah amiably said, 'of course they will be treated with care, and they will be cleaned, and the banknotes will be safely set aside from them.'

'Who will do all that?' Cedric asked.

'A young girl employed by Dorothy to help her keep the cottage dirt-free and tidy.'

'I hope she is well paid for it.'

'She is,' Zaniah assured him.

While Zaniah was having her shower Cedric wandered along the upstairs landing and passed three bedrooms, all of them with their doors open. Dorothy evidently believed in keeping her cottage adequately ventilated as well as clean and tidy. The first two rooms both contained a double bed, and he supposed these were spare rooms which various friends of hers could use on occasional visits to her. The third room, with a single bed in it, he assumed to be her own. And at the end of the passage there was a convenience he was glad to be able to take advantage of now. Just before he emerged from it a sudden vivid remembrance came to him of his Godmother Norma's two spare bedrooms, both single-bedded.

He was released from this rather sad remembrance by the voice of Dorothy commandingly calling, 'When are you two coming down to eat the meal I've been keeping warm in the oven for you?'

•

Zaniah and Cedric, who followed her rapid descent of the stairs a little cautiously, were soon occupying the seats at the kitchen table which were indicated to each of them by Dorothy.

'This is one of my home-made vegetarian pizzas,' she said, bringing it out of the oven on a large round plate and placing it in front of them. Then she produced three smaller plates which she had been warming on the rack above the oven, and gave one to Cedric and one to Zaniah, keeping the third for herself. 'You are allowed to use fingers if you like, but you'll find it rather hot, and there are knives and forks on the table here. The main problem is the geometrical one of cutting a circular pizza fairly into three equal parts.' She was successful, however, or at least she claimed to be, and Cedric and Zaniah sincerely praised her pizza, as they also did the ice-cream after it, which she assured them was made from real cream.

•

'You two must have had a hard day, I'm sure,' she said when they'd all three finished their meal, 'and the best thing you can do now is to go upstairs and get a good night's sleep.'

'May I help you with the washing-up first?' Zaniah asked.

'No,' Dorothy said peremptorily, 'but thanks for the offer.'

•

Cedric, after they'd reached the upstair landing, asked Zaniah quietly enough (he hoped) to avoid being overheard by Dorothy in the kitchen, 'Has she ever been married?'

'What a peculiar question,' Zaniah said. 'Why do you ask it?'

'Well, she gives me the impression of being somehow a bit innocent.'

'That's just her civilised politeness,' Zaniah said. 'She was in fact married, but her husband was killed in a traffic accident soon after their marriage. I'm sure she grieved genuinely for him, and she never married again, yet I doubt whether she has remained an unconsoled widow.'

'You mean she's had *affaires*?'

'Put it that way, if you like, though I can't be certain.'

'Would she disapprove, do you think,' Cedric suddenly dared to ask, 'if we didn't use both beds?'

'No. Perhaps she might even be grateful to us for saving her the expense of having two pairs of sheets and pillow cases laundered,' Zaniah said ironically. 'But aren't you being rather bold, Cedric? You are propositioning me, aren't you? Don't look so sheepish about it. Let me set your mind at rest by promising that you are going to have me "bolt upright" – I've not forgotten this appealing Chaucerian phrase I picked up at my university – in your arms tonight.'

They were now sitting close together on one of the double beds.

'There is something else I ought to tell you about,' Zaniah said. 'I have a perversion – or so it would be regarded by a majority of "normal" people.'

'I hope this doesn't mean you're a sadist,' Cedric said. 'I certainly wouldn't enjoy being physically hurt by you.'

'No, I'm neither a sadist nor a masochist,' Zaniah said. 'I am simply a gerontophile. And you and I will not be committing incest as my father and I would have been if he had allowed the mutual love between us to become sexual.'

'Have you thought about our taking precautions?' Cedric asked.

'There'll be no need for "precautions",' she said. 'Quite a while ago I had my ovaries removed after a cyst was detected in one of them.'

'So that's that,' he said, 'but now tell me: Is your gerontophilism promiscuous?'

'It isn't. I shall be faithful to you, Cedric, for as long as you live.'

'I trust in you absolutely, Zaniah, but I do wonder whether for any other lovers a conversation like this of ours has served as a foreplay leading up to the real thing.'

Soon after he had said this they flung off their dressing-gowns and she leaped and he tumbled into the bed. She quickly drew him down upon her. Then abruptly he pulled the bed-clothes up over them both, the absurd thought having come to him that supposing Dorothy were to catch them in flagrante delicto at this moment it wouldn't startle her quite as much as if she were to see them completely naked together.

•

He awoke slowly in the morning; and, half dreaming, he seemed to hear someone speaking the poet Shelley's lines, 'Rarely, rarely, comest thou, /Spirit of delight', and then almost fully awake he remembered parts of the final stanza in Shelley's poem: 'I love Love . . . But above all other things, Spirit, I love thee – . . . Oh, come, /Make once more my heart thy home.'

Suddenly he was wide awake with Zaniah awake beside him, and he was filled with an extreme joy such as had felt only once or twice previously in all his life. He told her of it, and she said she felt the same. Also she said that she had been awake before he had, and she added slyly, 'Perhaps I may have done something to cause you to have those dreams.'

They both laughed.

'Now we shall be able to go out invulnerably into a dangerous world,' he said.

'I don't know quite what you mean by that, but I do know that we mustn't be guilty of snoring at the breakfast table, like Uncle George and Auntie Mabel.'

'Where did you get that little old rhyme from?' Cedric asked.

'My boyfriend at the university,' she said.

•

They behaved well during breakfast, overcoming and completely hiding (they hoped) a powerful tendency they each had to doze off momentarily. By the end of breakfast, though, they were thoroughly awake.

Zaniah thanked Dorothy wholeheartedly for sheltering them both overnight, but startled her for an instant by adding, 'Now we must be on our travels again.'

Nevertheless, with what might have been a wink lasting no longer than half a second, Dorothy said, 'Lovers love to be together. Goodbye for now, my dears. See you again soon.'

They waved happily to her before they began walking away under a glorious sunnily blue springtime sky.

They walked hand in hand silently for a while until Zaniah, all at once remembering, asked Cedric, 'What did you mean when you said that now we shall be able to go out invulnerably into a dangerous world?'

'I think I must have meant that the best thing for our morale, in this undoubtedly dangerous world from which we can't escape, would be to persuade ourselves we're invulnerable.'

They were walking alongside a group of fir trees as Cedric said this, and to their extreme alarm a voice speaking from among the trees said, 'Cedric, that explanation you have given your charming companion isn't very convincing, I think.'

A tallish good-looking fair-haired man, in his early thirties perhaps, emerged from the trees.

'Don't you recognise me, Cedric?' he asked.

'I think I do,' Cedric said. 'Your name is Leonard, isn't it?'

'Yes, I'm Leonard Furnival. I was walking along this hill path and I happened to catch sight of you. I have been watching you both for some while. You looked like two angels, utterly happy. I felt an urge to give you a little surprise, and when you approached these trees in the course of your walk I hid behind them.'

Cedric said nothing.

Leonard went on, 'When you first met me I was a quantity surveyor employed by that odious construction firm Gamley & Tryst. I admitted I was ashamed of the work I was doing, and you asked why I didn't throw up the job. I knew you were right, and I did throw it up. Then I got the idea of creating what I called *The Little Theatre*. I had tried to live as an actor when I was a young man, but found I couldn't afford it. Here at last was a chance of my making a living by producing really good modern plays which would attract the permanent residents of that flourishing seaside town we both know so well.'

Cedric, remembering the scorn with which Leonard had treated his doubt then whether such plays would appeal to working-class people, now asked not quite unmaliciously, 'Was *The Little Theatre* a success?'

'No and yes,' Leonard answered. 'It failed while I was in charge of it, but it succeeded when it was taken over by someone I'd regarded as my friend and who to my regret produced mainly the crudest soft and not so soft porn in it.'

'I'm sorry,' Cedric sincerely said, 'and I hope you won't think I'm being impertinent in asking how you are earning your living now.'

'I am not earning a living now. I have saved enough money from serving firms like Gamley & Tryst to be able to pursue what I think of as a valuable hobby. There is a saying that money has no colour, and I never feel guilty in using it when I can to benefit honourable people such as your good selves.'

Neither of them made any comment, but he did not hesitate to continue, 'I have travelled many miles in this country, and I can reliably inform you which places are the least likely to be dangerous. I should mention that in order to avoid arrest by the police for being a beggar or a New Age vagrant, I call myself a freelance travel agent.'

'That doesn't recommend you to me, I'm afraid,' Zaniah not very seriously said. 'I've had the misfortune to encounter more than one far from reliable member of your profession.'

'Very well, will you agree to put me to a preliminary test by accompanying me to a nationally important event which could become dangerous but where with me as a guide we shall all three be unharmed?'

'You like to be mysterious, it seems,' Zaniah said, 'but yes, I will agree to accept your guidance.'

'And so will I,' Cedric a little hesitantly said.

'Good,' Leonard said, 'and now we have a mile and a half to walk, mostly along paths which have been common property for generations, though farmers are constantly trying to encroach on them, and we shall be doing our bit of public service by helping to keep them open.'

•

Soon after the beginning of their walk with him he asked Zaniah and Cedric, 'Did you start out this morning with any particular purpose in mind, or did you intend only to do a random ramble in the sun?'

Zaniah, answering for both Cedric and herself, told Leonard they'd intended to do a ramble, though on several previous occasions when she'd started with this intention she'd found something well worth investigating. She went on to tell him that she was a freelance investigative journalist. She expounded her political philosophy to him as they walked. He agreed with her that the world was in a state of chaos, but he didn't agree that the struggle to change it was worth while. 'It will always be the same,' he said.

Their argument continued until she and he and Cedric heard an outburst of male human yelling and cheering; and not long afterwards, as they reached the summit of a hill and could look downwards from it, they saw a high many-tiered football stadium which was divided into two separate sections at an angle to each other. These sections, Leonard was able to explain, were designed to keep the supporters of the opposing teams apart, and he added that at the bottom of each section wire fencing had been erected to prevent supporters or opponents of either team from getting on to the playing field; but as he spoke his two hearers became aware that a furious crowd inside one of the sections were pressing against their fence with such weight that they were forcing it down flat and they had begun to pour out on to the field.

• • •

'THIS IS IT,' Leonard said, 'the Cup Final between the Greys and the Mauves. The game seems just to have finished, and evidently the supporters of one of the teams are protesting about something. Let us hurry down and get as close to what's going on as we safely can.'

'Football has always bored me,' Zaniah said. 'It's an all-male sport, and whenever it appears while I'm watching telly I switch off.'

'Possibly you would not have found the present game enthralling, but I think that, as an investigative journalist, you might be considerably interested in what's now happening after it. Of course, there's no need for you to come down with me if you would rather not.'

'I'll come down with you,' she said; and Cedric, who apparently had been forgotten by Leonard temporarily, added – again somewhat hesitantly – 'And so will I.'

At the bottom of the hill Leonard exclaimed, 'Look, there's rioting and fire in the town to the right of us.' He was quiet for a moment, staring towards the flames. Then he said, 'My guess is that some would-be spectators who arrived too late to get tickets, or who were sold forged tickets by crooks, have just heard the result of the match and are expressing their feelings now.'

Leonard had no sooner finished speaking than to the left of him and Zaniah and Cedric a solitary man came running in their direction; and, glancing backwards over his shoulder as if he feared that he was being pursued, he collided quite heavily with them; but a moment before the collision he realised that his fears had been unfounded, and he became almost obsequiously apologetic.

'I am very, very sorry,' he said.

'Well,' Leonard said, 'I don't think much damage has been done to us.' He turned to Zaniah and Cedric and asked them, 'Has it?'

Zaniah answered for them both. 'Not much, I think,' she said, not knowing that Cedric felt a pain in his shoulder which might or might not mean that some damage had been done to it.

Leonard turned again to the man and, with a hint of condescension in his tone which Cedric did not like, he said, 'Can you tell us whether something happened during the game to start all this commotion after it?'

'Yes I can.'

'Good,' Leonard said. 'What's your name, by the way, if I may ask?'

'I am Fred Clewley,' the man said.

'Do you regularly attend football matches?'

'More regularly than I could before I lost my job as a hospital porter at a Trust hospital. The hospital was run into debt by the Management – or Mismanagement as some called them – and they closed down several wards to economise. Also they made me redundant, and I've been living on unemployment pay ever since.'

Leonard, without commenting on Fred Clewley's account of his own personal plight, said, 'Please carry on now, Fred, and tell us what happened in the game.'

'By half-time,' Fred Clewley said, 'the Greys and the Mauves had each scored one goal. Lavarello scored for the Greys – I daresay you've heard he cost the Club one and a half million – and Uhrmacher, who cost the Mauves just as much, scored the other. After half-time they both scored again, and the rest of their team members embraced them so hard that I wonder they weren't suffocated. But in the last minute of the game, when we were expecting a draw and a replay or an extra twenty minutes, Lavarello passed the ball back to his goalie who couldn't stop it, and an own-goal was scored. I think their supporters lynched both Lavarello and the goalie.'

'So that accounts for the commotion,' Leonard said grimly.

'Where are the police in all this, I wonder,' Zaniah said.

'Overwhelmed, I should think,' Leonard said, 'and phoning all over the country for reinforcements.'

Fred Clewley, less interested in police reinforcements than in continuing his story of the match, went on to say that for quite a while there were looks of satisfaction on the faces of some of the men who had taken part in the lynching, but others were quicker to realise that they could be charged with murder, found guilty, and sent to prison for years. In this mixed mood they heard the Mauve supporters wildly cheering because their team had won. The Grey supporters, goaded by the cheering, tried unsuccessfully to break down the wire fence in front of the section occupied by the Mauves; then the Mauves in retaliation started smashing their seats – gleefully knowing these to be the property of the Grey home club – and by flinging jagged seat-fragments down at the faces of their defeated opponents below.

•

'Has anything at all like this happened in England before?' Zaniah asked Leonard.

'I think not,' he said, 'but I believe an own-goal scorer was lynched in one of the South American countries, and the same sort of thing was just waiting to happen here.'

'And how will you save us from the town rioters now?' Cedric asked him.

'There can be only one way,' Leonard answered, 'uphill, though not by the same path we took when I led you down to get as near as we safely could to the fighting on the playing field after the lynching. Our problem now is to discover an uphill path quickly enough to escape being surrounded by the rioters and arsonists from the town. I think I can see a possible path. I confess I led you rather too close to danger on the football field, but I hope you will not be deterred by that from going up the path with me. I feel sure we cannot survive in any other way.'

Zaniah and Cedric did go with him, though the path was so steep that Cedric soon felt that if he climbed any farther, even with her help, he would be less likely to survive than to die of heart failure. Luckily, however, at the very moment when he decided that he could do no more climbing, the path became level. They had reached its summit. Leonard stopped; and Cedric did not need to be supported by Zaniah's arm beneath his now, though he was glad that she nevertheless still kept it there.

'The trees will prevent them from seeing us,' Leonard said, referring to the mob below, 'but we can see them.'

• • •

AN ALL-MALE GROUP varying in age from perhaps sixteen to forty had come upon an isolated thatch-roofed farmhouse, and were seizing and wringing the necks of hens and geese; and one of them, a young man, finding a rusty-looking sickle lying on the ground, lopped off the head of a hostile farm watchdog with it. Soon an old woman - she might just have woken from a short nap – came out of the farmhouse and was speechlessly appalled by what she saw. The young man yelled at her 'You mucky old sow.' Then one of the group's members who appeared to be aged between thirty and forty, and who possessed a smoker's lighter probably of a type containing compressed wool soaked in petrol, managed to set fire after several failed attempts to the thatch of the farmhouse roof.

•

Abruptly the whole gang of hen and goose thieves, together with the thatch arsonist, became simultaneously aware of something which caused them to hurry away from the farmhouse. Perhaps they had caught sight of a distant squad of policemen advancing in their direction.

'However, it looks as though they may not have physically molested the woman,' Leonard said. 'We must go down to her at once, and give her what help and comfort we can.'

'I'm afraid it would take me even longer to go down than it took me to come up,' Cedric said.

'That's true,' Zaniah said.

'So I must say goodbye to you both, and I regretfully doubt whether we three will ever meet again.'

He went almost bounding down the hill in the rapidly brightening light of the flaming thatched roof. Luckily an ambulance, alerted no doubt by the blaze, arrived within minutes. (The fire brigade did not come yet, presumably having fires still to deal with in the town.) Leonard and the driver lifted the woman gently on to a stretcher and into the ambulance, and he remained with her in the ambulance when the driver drove off on a quest, not likely to be brief, for a hospital uneconomising enough to be capable of providing a bed for her.

•

Cedric, watching from the level summit of the path as the ambulance below departed, allowed himself to imagine what the farm had been like in the woman's younger days. She'd had a husband, and together they had just about made a living out of farming, though it had cost them some cruelly hard work at times. But her husband died young, and she couldn't believe she would be able to carry on alone; nevertheless she did carry on – until today. She was a heroine.

•

Cedric described his imaginings to Zaniah, who said, 'And what do you suppose will happen to the poor woman when she's discharged from the hospital?'

'I suppose the local authorities will be bound by law not to leave her without shelter, and they'll put her in a bed-&-breakfast lodging house and make her an allowance of cash that they'll consider sufficient to meet her needs for the remainder of each day; but there is a horrible possibility that before long scouts from the bacon factory will find her and lure her away; and this will be the end of her.'

'And do you think we can do nothing to stop them?' Zaniah asked.

'If we tried, we would very soon get hung up as white carcases ourselves.'

'Yes, I'm afraid that's all too probable,' Zaniah agreed.

'Well, where are we going now?' Cedric asked. 'Is it to be a random ramble again?'

'I think it will have to be,' Zaniah said.

•

They took no notice of the autumn flowers in the fields beside the path they walked along, nor of the birds circling the clear blue sky above them, and they didn't even appreciate the fine weather they were lucky to be having. But after walking a couple of miles they came upon a solitary building which immediately excited Cedric's interest. It seemed to him to show a close exterior resemblance to the CAVE OF ENDOR pub; and when he told Zaniah that he couldn't briefly explain why it interested him so much but thought it would interest her too, she became keen to enter it with him at once.

•

Above the main entrance and at right angles to it a decorative iron bracket supported a slightly swinging square of painted metal with the words THE PUB CLUB printed on each side of it. Cedric pushed open the main entrance door and held it open for her to follow him into the bar-room.

He was startled by the appearance of one of the two barmaids there. She looked remarkably like the bacon factory receptionist, except that she seemed to have tarted herself up a bit. He would have gone to the bar and ordered drinks from her for Zaniah and himself, and he would have asked her if he was right in thinking she had been that receptionist, but suddenly from somewhere at the back of the bar a middle-aged man emerged who was instantly recognised by Cedric as his enemy, Goran; and Goran, conscious of being recognised, said, 'I know you must detest me, Cedric, and with good reason.'

Ingrained bourgeois politeness made Cedric disingenuously give his face a deprecatory look, as if he disclaimed having any reason not to like Goran.

Goran, ignoring this politeness, said to Cedric that there was something he wanted to let him know now which he thought would considerably interest him.

Cedric said nothing, and Goran began: 'I was still running my hotel in Brandsbrook when I had an unusual visitor who stayed only for a weekend, and just before leaving he told me in strict confidence he was a member of an undercover Government agency – not MI5 or MI6 but a more important one, NF7, never heard of by the general public, and it was under the full control of the real rulers of this country. He said he was not permitted to reveal his actual name to me but only the number that the agency had allotted him, 38, which happened to be approximately my age at that time. He told me I would be well paid for any information I could pass on to him about a young man named Cedric Durcombe, a schoolmaster who was known to have visited the Soviet Union and who might be able to exert a subversive influence on some of his older pupils.'

'I'm certainly interested to hear this,' Cedric said in a somewhat mollified tone, which evidently encouraged Goran to go on to tell him, 'You may also be interested to know that NF7 has lately turned against me and stopped all payments to me. I suspect my wife may in some way have helped to bring this about. Perhaps you remember she had recently left me at the time when I first met you.'

'Yes, I do,' Cedric said.

Suddenly, very emotionally, Goran told him and Zaniah, 'I am in terrible trouble now.'

They were silent, and he went on, 'If you will come with me into the lounge at the back of this pub where we can talk in comfort I will tell you a true story I think you won't easily forget.'

They followed him, and he mentioned that the supple dark green leather covering of the sofa he invited them to sit on had a layer of highest quality foam-rubber upholstery beneath it.

'This comfortable sofa must have been very expensive,' Cedric commented.

'It was,' Goran said. 'Una and I – she is my partner and you will have seen her serving at the bar when you first came in – Una and I wanted our "PUB CLUB" to be upmarket. We wanted our customers to be able sit in this lounge for instance and drink their coffees and liqueurs and smoke perhaps a Havana cigar or two, or to play snooker on the brand-new full-sized billiard table we've had installed in another room, or to play card games in a third room which I would specially like to show you. It is the largest of the three. It could be – and I hope it will be – used occasionally for dances. Follow me and you shall see it.'

As soon as they were inside the room with him he asked, 'But where are the card tables?'

Cedric and Zaniah, aware that this was a merely rhetorical question, said nothing and were led by him to look at a flat oblong piece of polished brown wood close to the wall of the room. He pulled the oblong piece towards him out from its contact with the wall and turned it upwards till a dark brown pillar standing on a similarly coloured wooden base – which was supported by four wooden claws pointing north, east, south, and west, as it were – swung down into view.

'HEY PRESTO,' Goran said, swivelling the oblong top of the table and revealing packs of playing cards in a compartment underneath this. He then closed the top and lifted a table-leaf which when he hinged it over formed a complete red cloth table-top ready for the players.

'How many of these fascinating tables have you got?' Cedric asked.

'Six. They are fakes, of course, I bought them almost for a song from an antiques dealer who thought they were quite out of fashion.'

'But they didn't cost you nothing,' Zaniah boldly said, 'nor could all the other admirable alterations you are making to this pub.'

'True enough,' Goran said.

'May I be so crude as to ask how you've financed all these improvements?' Zaniah asked.

'By borrowing from a friendly bank. My favourite maxim in financial matters has always been, "Never use your own money". But the disaster that has come upon Una and myself has nothing to do with finance.'

He paused; then, inconsequentially it seemed, he added, 'Una and I have always adhered strictly to the rule that all customers must be off the premises by closing time, and it was closing time almost immediately after your arrival, so there were no customers to hinder me from exhibiting the lounge and the card-players' room to you.'

Cedric and Zaniah waited for him to continue talking; but a rasping clearance of choking phlegm from his throat, which quite alarmed them, was apparently necessary to him before he could speak again.

'Late in the evening recently,' he said, 'two plain-clothes police detectives, a male and a female, called on me here. They showed me their badges and told me they they wanted a word with me. I led them into the lounge. I thought they'd possibly been misinformed by someone that we had been allowing particular friends of ours in for drinks after closing-time. But I soon found how wrong I was.'

'We have been here in plain clothes once before, as ordinary customers,' the female said.

'And we got the impression,' the male said, 'that your PUB CLUB is really a brothel. It is, isn't it?'

'Of course it isn't,' I said.

'We happen to know that your barmaid Trudy is a prostitute who entertains customers of yours in a bedroom upstairs here,' the female detective said.

'Worse still,' the male said, 'we have ascertained that one of your customers is a paedophile and that Trudy has been supplying him with children to abuse. This is an offence for which not only Trudy and the paedophile, but also you, Mr Goran, in whose so-called PUB CLUB it has been occurring, will undoubtedly receive a lengthy custodial sentence, and during it you will be lucky if the other prisoners, all of them violently intolerant of sexual offenders, fail to assault and perhaps permanently injure you.'

'You can imagine the fear I felt,' Goran said to Cedric. 'But the next day the two detectives returned, and the male said to me that on one condition, if I would agree to it, no prosecution would be brought against me or my partner Una. This condition was that I should consent to allowing him and his female colleague to have sex with Una, who had become very attractive to them in their differing ways. I said nothing. But the male said that silence meant consent.'

'I heard afterwards from Una of the vile practices she was being made to endure. On each occasion the female fetched an eiderdown from a bedroom upstairs and laid it out over part of the billiard table. Then the two of them lifted her quickly on to the eiderdown, and the female – a powerfully built butch-type dyke – forcibly held her down exactly in the positions he desired while he repeatedly violated her, and after this he was similarly helpful to the female while she satisfied her requirements which Una found even more repulsive.

'And it will all happen again and again,' Goran despairingly said. 'Oh Cedric, Oh Zaniah what am I to do? Can you help me?'

'Yes, I think I can,' Zaniah said. 'I just don't for one moment believe that Trudy is a prostitute or that a paedophile frequenting your PUB CLUB gets supplies from her of children he can abuse – this is nothing but a monstrous vicious calumny, and I think you will be able to make its perpetrators pay heavily for it.'

'How can I do that?' Goran doubtingly asked.

'Expose these bent police-detectives. Tell the whole story, or as much of it as you think wise, to whichever tabloid newspaper will pay the largest sum for the exclusive right to publish it.'

'Oh thank you, thank you, I can't thank you enough for that helpful suggestion,' Goran said: but the humble gratitude in his voice did little to lessen Cedric's dislike of him.

'Una and I will be able to feel much more hopeful tonight,' Goran said.

'But we shall have to leave you now,' Zaniah said.

'No, no, you can't go tonight,' Goran said. 'Rain is deluging down and you would get soaked through.'

'Perhaps we shall; although we've both got raincoats. Nothing could induce me to stay any longer in your PUB CLUB. So I have to say goodbye Mr - what is your first name, by the way?'

'Harvey,' Goran said.

'Well, goodbye Mr Harvey Goran,' Zaniah said, and Cedric said the same, though he couldn't resist adding not altogether unironically, 'Better luck next time.'

•

'Where shall we go to?' Cedric asked Zaniah after they'd come out from the PUB CLUB into the frantically wild wet night.

'I don't know,' she said.

'It will have to be yet another random walk then,' he said; and she agreed.

Their raincoats, guaranteed to be shower-proof, became all too soon entirely useless as a protection against the heavily pelting rain, and Cedric and Zaniah were both drenched to the skin.

•

'I can't go on,' Cedric shouted – or, rather, he tried to shout. But Zaniah heard him and shouted back, 'You can and will.'

And with her arm beneath his he found he could. The wet against his skin seemed less cold after a while; but eventually, although he continued to walk, he was beginning to drop into a trance-like drowsiness when, all of a sudden, Zaniah exclaimed, 'See what we've arrived at! My "safe house" - Dorothy's cottage.'

•

They both stood still. 'If I could believe in telepathy,' Zaniah said, 'I would be sure that Dorothy had telepathically guided us here, where subconsciously I've been wanting to go all the time since we left the PUB CLUB. And look, the lights have come on in her cottage, and she is opening her front door to us.'

•

'Didn't I tell you when I last said goodbye to you that I would be seeing you both again soon?' Dorothy asked.

'Yes, you did,' Zaniah said.

'And what a state you are both in now. Soaked and filthy and I daresay half starving. Come in, come in; and get upstairs to shower yourselves at once.'

They staggeringly obeyed, though Cedric didn't know how he managed it.

They shared a shower together, found towels to dry with and dressing-gowns to put on after that.

'Decency at last,' Zaniah said; and Cedric knew that she was not using this word merely to refer to their having covered their nakedness after showering themselves.

•

They came downstairs and found Dorothy in her kitchen, stirring something in a large saucepan.

'Asparagus soup,' she said. 'Out of a tin. It's been in my cupboard for quite a while. But there's nothing wrong with it.'

'I'm sure it will be delicious,' Zaniah said.

'Very well, lay the table. And you'll find some cherry and vanilla yoghurt in the fridge. Don't just stand there watching me stir the soup.'

'I'm sorry, Dorothy.'

'I was only joking, of course. I know how tired you must be. Sit down at the table, both of you, immediately.'

•

She served them, and they ate greedily, and having finished they sincerely praised her cooking.

'What will you have to drink?' she asked.

'Oh, just water, please,' Cedric said, and Zaniah said she'd like water too.

Dorothy filled two mugs from the drinking-water tap at the kitchen sink – she proudly made a point of telling Cedric and Zaniah that the water was drinking-water.

In spite of the rain they'd so recently been drenched by, they drank thirstily, and they could have drunk the water from the non-drinking-water tap just as thirstily

•

'Up to bed now at once,' Dorothy ordered them, 'and stay there as long as ever you like.'

They said goodnight to her, and they tried to go up the stairs as though they were doing so with the utmost ease.

•

They woke rather late in the morning, but they talked as they got dressed.

'Decency,' Cedric said.

'Yes, Dorothy has it.'

'And many other people in the world have it, men, women and children of all races and classes.'

'And many have not got it,' Zaniah said. 'Not so very many, but these still have power over the others.'

'Shelley's battle-cry, "Ye are many, They are few," was a good one,' Cedric said, 'but ours at present has got to be, "Decency is not enough", which echoes Nurse Edith Cavell's heroic saying.'

' "Decency is not enough" could become a heroic saying for us,' Zaniah unexplainingly suggested.

Cedric felt that she did not want to explain it now, and that perhaps she wasn't clear yet what she herself meant by it.

'Well anyway we know it is true,' he said.

'I think Dorothy also knows this,' Zaniah said. 'But we mustn't overdo our lateness for breakfast. Let us go down as soon as we can.'

•

Dorothy gave them porridge and milk and butter and bread and marmalade and tea, though she herself had only a bowl of bread and milk.

'This is my usual breakfast,' she told them. Then she added, 'You are going to leave me today, I think.'

'Yes, Dorothy, we have our duty to do,' Zaniah said.

•

Zaniah and Cedric were sad when they kissed her goodbye at her door; and this time she did not say to them, 'See you again soon.'

• • •

'IS THIS TO BE another random walk?' Cedric asked as they left Dorothy's cottage behind them.

'I haven't really thought about that yet. Perhaps it shouldn't be.'

'Randomness can have very useful results,' Cedric said, 'as when it took us to Goran's Pub Club where we were able to expose those two police crooks.'

'Yes, but far worse crimes than theirs are committed by the rulers of this country,' Zaniah said, 'and since we won't live for ever we ought perhaps to target these immediately instead of waiting for them to be randomly exposed.'

'Are you thinking of armament sales, for instance?'

'No. But now something more in your line suggests itself to me.'

'What?'

'Schools – of all types.'

'Where?'

'Obviously we can't visit schools throughout the whole country,' Zaniah said; 'and we would be absurdly overreaching ourselves if, simply because we happen to be in the south-west now, we were to aim at investigating most of the schools betweeen Devon and Dorset.'

'Of course,' Cedric said. 'So what is your solution?'

'We need to think of a single centre of population where all types of school could be found.'

'What about Ashester?'

'Too ecclesiastical, perhaps,'

'Or Helibridge. It's industrial, but mainly in the latest modern way. No smoke or chemical poisons, and quite a bit of general culture of an inoffensive kind.'

•

They tried to keep to well-trodden public paths as they discussed which of these centres would be the better one to investigate. No stinking car-infested roads for them. Nor attractive-looking country lanes either, where at sharp bends large farm vehicles could loom up at any moment.

They felt they were lucky to find fairly soon an unhedged path that led over a wide stubbly field and helped them to carry on their discussion with minimal attention to their surroundings – until they came to a footbridge which spanned the double lines of a railway. They saw, however, that on the far side of the bridge there was another hedgeless path, and they decided to go over the bridge to get to this.

But when they were half-way over they stopped to watch an express train which came suddenly rushing out from under where they were standing; and to their horror when it had reached a distance of about half a mile ahead they saw it crash into the carriages of another fast moving train.

With trepidation they agreed to go and see exactly what had happened there.

They resumed their walk across to the far side of the footbridge. Then they turned to go westward and to move as quickly as they could through long grass beside the railway till they were close enough to see ambulances that had already arrived, and blood that had dripped over the wreckage-strewn ground, and men carrying injured or dying railway passengers on stretchers to the ambulances.

•

Out of a cottage several hundred yards away from the accident a man with a slight stoop and wearing a somewhat grubby cloth cap emerged and came towards them.

'Might you be journalists?' he asked, in a peculiar accent which was like an amalgam of various differing British accents.

While Zaniah was beginning to answer this man, Cedric suddenly remembered a happening early on in the Second World War. He and a fellow left-winger named Walter Paget were out at night delivering anti-war leaflets to houses in a working-class street. What they were doing was before long discovered by a copper's nark, a small cloth-capped man, who hurried away to bring a policeman to them, and the policeman quite politely said to Paget, 'May I see your Identity Card, sir?'

'Oh, but Officer you have absolutely no right to ask that,' Paget opportunely answered. The policeman, uncertain (these Cards had only very recently been introduced), returned to the police station, no doubt to consult the sergeant there. Meanwhile Walter Paget and Cedric Durcombe speedily and thankfully escaped from the street, and each soon got safely back to his own wartime billet.

•

Now Cedric, wondering whether their cloth-capped questioner might be some kind of nark, asked him bluntly, 'Would you mind telling us your name?'

The man, firmly evasive, answered, 'I go by the name of Paxton.' Then he added, 'And what names do you go by?'

'Our real names,' Zaniah said, and she told him what these were.

'You described yourself to me just now,' he said to Zaniah, 'as a freelance investigative journalist.'

'Yes,' she said.

'Do you know the names of the two privatised railway companies whose executives will be especially interested in this accident?'

'No, I don't,' she said.

'One of the companies is ROLLING-STOCK and the other is SIGNALS. You have possibly heard of them.'

'I think I may have,' she said.

'The accident happened where two sets of rails cross,' Paxton went on to tell her.

'Is there some sort of level crossing there?' Cedric asked.

'Yes, though without gates of course. It's an old-fashioned and dangerous arrangement which neither of the two privatised companies has been willing to pay the cost of modernising. A bridge would have solved the problem.'

'Does this mean that you disapprove of privatisation?' Zaniah asked.

'I never said so,' Paxton answered. 'And now we come to the big question,' he continued: 'Was the signal at green or red when the driver crashed his train into the other train? The SIGNALS Company is believed to have insisted that it was at red, and as the driver had remarkably received only slight injuries, they got the police to arrest him immediately. But,' Paxton added, 'the ROLLING-STOCK Company is said to have asserted that it was at green, and that SIGNALS are to blame.' He paused portentously, then suddenly he told Zaniah and Cedric, 'If you could say the signal was at red your reward would be considerable.

'But neither of us saw it,' Zaniah said.

'That doesn't matter. The reward would be a five figure one.'

'So you are prepared to bribe us?'

'Yes.'

'In hard cash?' Cedric asked.

'Certainly.'

To their amazement he produced from a bulging pocket of his grubby jacket a huge wad of banknotes.

'No, Mr Paxton, we are unbribable,' Zaniah told him.

'You prigs,' he said.

•

They turned and walked away from him, and as they walked Zaniah said, 'I wonder which company he works for.'

'ROLLING-STOCK is my guess,' Cedric said. 'Though I expect they'll go to Law about it and a six figure sum at least will be paid by the company that judgment is pronounced against.'

'Or it will all be settled out of court,' Zaniah said, 'and the maimed and the relatives of the killed will get nothing, or if they are paid anything it will be a mere pittance. But I am only conjecturing. I realise how little I know about the workings of the Law.'

'I know just as little,' Cedric said. 'We ought – and you as an investigative journalist especially ought – to get to know a lot more about it.'

'You're right,' Zaniah said, 'though now we must let nothing divert us any longer this morning from starting to investigate private schools.'

After they'd walked on for a short distance Cedric said, 'I'm not feeling well,' and he sat down heavily on the well-trodden public path. Soon she sat down beside him. 'I feel bad too,' she said.

'What do you think could be causing it?' he asked.

'I've no idea,' she said.

'I don't suppose we've been poisoned by happening to brush up against the leaves of a giant hogweed.'

'No, there weren't any hogweeds about, not even small ones.'

'We could be feeling delayed shock from seeing those ghastly railway accident casualties,' he suggested.

'That seems more possible,' she said.

•

Within a few minutes they began to feel a little better and at last they were able to help each other to stand up.

'Delayed shock was the cause,' Cedric said, 'and it could come again, like the second wave of an earthquake.'

'Possibly it could, but it hasn't yet,' Zaniah said; 'so now we should set about finding schools to investigate this morning as we intended to.'

• • •

HELIBRIDGE WAS THE CENTRE of population which they found themselves nearing. They assumed this when they saw its chimneyless modern factory buildings; and as they approached one of these they noticed close beside it what was unmistakably a school.

They heard a noise of shouting and screeching and laughing and they saw an asphalted playground overcrowded with children.

'Why can't they be let out on to the field at the far end of their playground?' Zaniah wondered.

'Because apparently whoever owns that field – a farmer perhaps – has chosen to put barbed wire fencing all round it.'

As Cedric said this he suddenly remembered how in his long-ago teaching days a colleague of his named McCloy had quietened a class that was becoming restless and inattentive. McCloy had climbed on to his chair and then on to the master's desk, and reaching up to the white glass lampshade above him he had unscrewed the electric bulb from its socket under the shade, looked frowningly at it for a moment or two, rescrewed it into its socket, got down from the desk and sat in his chair again. The ruse worked admirably and he was able to carry on the lesson with no further restlessness or inattention among the boys.

'Lend me your rucksack,' he said to Zaniah.

'What for?'

'I want to get into the middle of those children and to stand on it and to address them.'

'You certainly shan't have it,' she said. 'It's got food in it which would be crushed and spoilt if you stood on it. And in any case you are quite tall enough to be able to go among them and address them with nothing but the asphalt of the playground to stand on.'

'All right, I'll do that,' he said.

•

Cedric, looking serious though not unfriendly, made his way through the crowding children to what was more or less the centre of the playground, and then he abruptly stopped. With a raised forefinger he pointed up as if in amazement at the cloudless sky. 'Do you see it?' he asked the children.

They all stared at the sky and, after a while, one of them asked, respectfully enough, 'See what, Sir?'

'The Blue, the Blue,' Cedric said. 'Why is the sky Blue? What would it look like if you could see it from the moon? Ask your teacher at the end of break.'

•

Almost immediately after he'd said this a tall gaunt-faced man holding a large brass bell by its brown wooden handle came out on to the playground from the open doorway of what was presumably a classroom. He shook the bell, causing it to ring twice, and the children obediently formed up into line and marched into the classroom, while their bell-ringing teacher remained outside. He spoke pleasantly to Cedric: 'Am I right in guessing from your performance that you and I are members of the same profession?'

'Yes,' Cedric sympathetically answered, 'or, rather, I was. I retired some years ago.'

'Lucky man!' the present teacher exclaimed; then he added, 'But I wouldn't like you to think that my saying so means I am unhappy teaching here. I'm not. I'm very happy, and so is my wife who teaches the infants in a smaller building close to this one. The trouble is that the County Council have decided that all village schools under their control are to be shut down, and the pupils from these are to be brought together in one large new building as soon as the construction firm has finished work on it.'

'I suppose the Council's idea is to save money,' Cedric said.

'Yes, partly that,' the teacher said.

'And I suppose,' Zaniah said, 'it's not unlikely that the contract has been concluded with a firm in which one of the Councillors has a personal interest?'

'Quite likely,' the teacher said, 'though it might not be easy to prove this.'

'And what about the infants?' Cedric asked.

'I expect it will be argued that some of them are too old to be regarded as infants any longer and should join the other children in the new building,' the teacher said, 'and as for those who most obviously aren't too old, they can stay at home with mother – or with grandmother – if mother has to go out to do a poorly paid job because she desperately needs the money.'

•

'I suppose,' Cedric said, 'there are parents who, though not at all well-off, are prepared to make sacrifices in order to pay for their children to be privately taught. Could you say what the attitude of the councillors is towards such parents?'

'The majority of the councillors are delighted with them, of course,' the teacher said, 'just as they are delighted to farm off any public service (refuse collection, for instance) to the highest private bidder. But they are only imitating in a small way the behaviour of the Government itself, which sells outrageously underpriced public assets to private entrepreneurs, and has even encouraged them to establish private prisons.'

'I can see that you are a man after our own hearts,' Zaniah said, smiling.

'It's good to meet people who share my and my wife's views,' the teacher said. 'There aren't all that many of us, not yet, though I've never doubted there will be in the harder times to come.'

'What are you going to do when your village school is shut down?' Zaniah asked.

'I don't think the Council will have the nerve simply to forget our existence,' the teacher said. 'They'll probably send us to the toughest of their schools. And what will the two of you be doing, if I may ask?'

'We shall investigate private schools, I expect,' Zaniah said, 'especially the type of school which has a headmistress with a dubious degree, and assistants with none, and which claims to be able to educate pupils from the ages of five to sixteen.'

The teacher smiled. 'Well, I wish you luck,' he said, 'and whatever happens to my wife and myself I shall not forget you.'

'Whatever happens to Cedric and me,' Zaniah said, 'I hope we shall remember you and try to live up to your example.'

'Goodbye now,' the teacher said, 'and thanks for your kindly high opinion of me.'

They shook hands.

Cedric and Zaniah then turned and walked away from him without looking back.

•

'I don't imagine we'll ever meet him again,' Cedric said.

'No,' Zaniah agreed, 'neither in this world or the next – and by next I mean the even more appalling world which threatens to come next into existence on the earth.'

•

They hadn't been walking on for long before they heard the roar of aircraft flying quite low over their heads.

'Those are fighter-bombers, I think,' Cedric said, believing he had seen somewhat similar aircraft during the Second World War.

'They ought to be stopped at once from practising low flights over the heads of civilians,' Zaniah said indignantly.

'I'm not so sure it is practice they are doing,' Cedric said.

'What do you mean?' Zaniah asked.

'I mean that for some months the most powerful nation in the world has been threatening to drop its very latest most accurate missiles on to yet another small nation whose leader has disobeyed it,' Cedric said, 'and I mean that the toadying Government under which we live has servilely offered its support to the threateners. Perhaps the attack has started at this very moment.'

'If it has,' Zaniah said, 'what do you think we should about it?'

'Well, we can at least express our utter opposition to it when we get into conversation with some of the people we are soon going to meet.'

'The people we're going to meet,' Zaniah said, 'will all be involved in private education, which we intend to investigate, and I suspect they'll be far keener to defend themselves than to listen to any political statement from us.'

'That's true,' Cedric admitted.

'Excuse me,' a voice suddenly said, 'but I happened to overtake you as I was doing my usual constitutional morning walk, and I couldn't help hearing what you were talking about.'

'Oh,' Zaniah said, with more than a hint of resentment in her tone.

She turned and saw beside her a man who so nearly resembled Paxton that she was later to name him 'the Paxton-Clone' when she spoke of him to Cedric.

The Paxton-Clone did not allow himself to be put off by Zaniah's uninviting tone. 'I could tell you things about private education in this district which I think you and your friend ought to know – and to publicise. Would you like me to?'

After a brief hesitation she said, 'Yes.'

• • •

'I'LL BEGIN WITH one of the most prestigious of all our private – or should I say "Public" schools, which is what they call themselves,' Paxton-Clone said. 'Let's give it the name Crampton. Much of the wood inside its six ancient "Houses" is so fungus-infected and worm-eaten that foreign tourists visiting it find difficulty in understanding why the British aristocracy choose to send their sons to such a school. And quite near to it is an equally antiquated church which these sons have to attend briefly every weekday, and for two hours every Sunday.'

'I wonder whether some of the bolder pupils sometimes decide to cut the Sunday service and to spend two hours in ways they find more pleasant,' Cedric said.

'You wonder correctly,' Paxton-Clone said. 'However, they risk being caught and sadistically thrashed by the prefects.'

'Don't they sometimes try to take revenge for that?' Zaniah asked.

Paxton-Clone, without answering her, said, 'I think you had better come with me to see the actual school and church.'

•

They agreed to go with him.

•

He did not take them inside the school buildings. He explained that these were all locked up because of the half-term holiday which had just begun. Nor did he take them inside the church. 'It too is locked,' he said. 'A valuable miniature painting has lately been stolen from the high altar, and I should have to ask the Rector - a man I detest - for the key. But I think that the sight merely of the exteriors of the buildings and of the church may help your minds to visualise the horrors I want to tell you about.'

Cedric and Zaniah looked at him with suspicion. Was this man, for a purpose no doubt advantageous to himself, hoping to convince them that something supernatural had happened here?

Paxton-Clone ignored their look, and began telling his horror story:

'Not so long ago the Rector of this parish felt that the grass in the church graveyard had grown unduly long, and he hired a yokel to scythe it down. This man, having finished his job, and having been meagrely paid for it by the notoriously wealthy and miserly Rector, reported to him that three of the gravestones had been knocked down and that there was a pile of brown earth heaped up close to each of these, and that open graves could be seen which had smashed coffins and decaying corpses in them; though the heads of the corpses were missing.'

Paxton-Clone waited for some comment from Cedric or from Zaniah. He got none. Nevertheless he continued:

'The respectable Rector, who was scared that he might be held responsible for what had happened, hastily informed the local police. They, however, were quite unable to trace the coffin-smashers or the missing heads, and had to appeal to the national police for help. But these also, in spite of spending thousands of pounds on dredging rivers and hacking down trees, were totally unsuccessful. The mystery might never have been solved if one of the cleaning women at Crampton, noticing a peculiarly unpleasant smell, hadn't discovered the heads wrapped in newspaper in the bedside cupboards of three of the boys. The boys were expelled, of course, but in order to preserve the reputation of this famous "Public" school the whole thing was hushed up.'

• • •

'WHY DID YOU hate the Rector so much?' Zaniah suddenly asked.

Paxton-Clone was taken by surprise, and hesitated for more than a moment before saying, 'He accused me of having stolen the miniature painting from the high altar.'

'Had you stolen it?' Zaniah coolly asked.

'Certainly not,' Paxton-Clone angrily answered.

'Did you sue him for slander?' Cedric asked, not quite sure that 'slander' was the right legal word to use.

'No. I wouldn't have stood a chance of winning against him. He is rich and could have afforded to employ the most expensive lawyers. What's more, the judge, being of the same social class as he is would have tended to be biased against me. And I very much doubt whether I would even have been able to get "legal aid". Few barristers, if they're any good, find this pays them enough nowadays.'

Cedric and Zaniah were silent for a while, and so was Paxton-Clone. At last, he said quite cheerfully, 'Well, I'll take you along now to investigate some of our leading private "Prep" schools, mostly just as expensive as the "Public" schools they prepare boys for.'

'What about girls?' Zaniah asked.

'I'll admit I know almost nothing about private girls' schools, or about private co-educational schools for that matter. But I could take you to a boys' Prep school run by a man named Bevan who has got himself both nationally and internationally well-known as an advanced educational theorist.'

'I've read one of his books,' Cedric said.

'What did you think of it?' Paxton-Clone asked.

'Not much,' Cedric said.

'I could tell you something about him which very few people know.'

'What?' Zaniah asked.

'When the older boys reach puberty he "baptises" them by getting them to jump naked into the bath with him.'

Neither Zaniah nor Cedric made any comment about this.

'I think it would be very much worth your while to look into the life-style of this Mr Bevan,' Paxton-Clone said to Zaniah.

'I disagree,' Zaniah said.

'But it is your duty as an investigative journalist to investigate this man,' he said.

Cedric turned on him angrily, saying, 'We don't need you to tell us what our duty is.'

He took Zaniah's arm and they walked unhesitatingly away, leaving Paxton-Clone behind them.

•

After they had been walking in silence for a short while Zaniah said, 'That was good – he had become an intrusive bore – but your vehemence surprised me.'

'Perhaps this is because you haven't known me quite long enough to realise how paranoid I can be about spies and secret service agents. It started with the Cold War at the end of World War Two. Anyone known to have serious left-wing sympathies was likely to be under surveillance.'

'Do you think Paxton-Clone was a spy?'

'Well, there's a saying that may amuse you: "Just because you're paranoid doesn't mean they aren't watching you." '

Zaniah laughed.

'Oh dear, I'm feeling so tired,' Cedric said.

'We've had a long day,' she said.

'And evening's coming on and we're miles from any place where we could stay the night.'

'Never mind,' she said, smiling. 'We'll just have to wrap ourselves in a groundsheet I have with me and go to sleep in a wood.'

And this is what they in fact did.

Both of them slept very soundly. Only after Cedric had completely woken did the thought come to him that insects such as spiders and large woodland ants could have been crawling over him while he'd slept. He jumped up and shook himself.

Zaniah, awakened by this, also stood up quickly, but it was not any thought of insects that came into her mind then. It was an idea, exciting to her, which she expressed to him by saying: 'Investigation is not enough.'

'Why not?' he asked her.

'An investigation which revealed an anti-human crime, for instance, wouldn't in itself be enough. It would need to be followed by action against the criminal.'

'Well, yes, that seems pretty obvious.'

'But the point is that such revelations so often aren't followed by action.'

There was a sudden roar of numerous aircraft not very high above them in the almost cloudless sky.

'They are at it again,' Cedric said. 'Those planes look like fighter-bombers, I think; and most probably the Government intends them to attack one of the sides in one of the present African or Balkan civil wars.'

'You sound almost as if you are getting bored with it,' Zaniah said. 'We mustn't ever forget that we here could, sooner than we expect, become involved in a civil war ourselves.'

'Do you think it's possible that the Irish, the Scots, the Welsh and perhaps the Cornish too, might actually be capable of combining to make war against the English?'

'No, I don't,' she said.

'Of course I'm not serious in seeming to be unsure of the kind of civil war you are really thinking of. It is class war.'

'Yes,' she said, 'and what we need to investigate next is the extent to which conscious class antagonism exists at present.'

'I suspect it may be more conscious among the bosses than among the workers,' Cedric said. 'But listen, I think I can hear a voice speaking through a megaphone in the the town just ahead of us. It could be a policeman's. Or it could be a politician's.'

•

They soon reached the outer ranks of a large crowd, mostly of men, who were beginning to shout back at a megaphone-holding man standing high on the roof of a vehicle parked in the midst of them and pleadingly addressing them.

Cedric after a short while understood that the man was a trade union official trying to persuade them to accept a reduction in pay proposed by the management. 'If we were to refuse,' he said, 'the whole factory would have to be closed down. It would no longer bring in any profit to the owners.'

This simple economic statement roused the fury of the crowd, who then rushed towards the vehicle on which the speaker was standing. He was saved only by the quick intervention of the police. Their batons were conspicuous at their belts as they surrounded the vehicle and helped the speaker down from it. They led him through the crowd to a waiting police car and drove him away.

Then one of the men climbed up on to the top of the vehicle and loudly shouted out the word STRIKE!

Instantly and furiously and more and more loudly the crowd – which seemed to be growing larger every moment – bawled out again and again this word STRIKE STRIKE STRIKE STRIKE . . .

Suddenly Cedric realised that Zaniah was no longer with him. A terrible fear came irresistibly upon him. He felt as if he was all alone in the world. But within minutes she re-appeared and came to him.

'There's no need for you to look so bleak, my darling. I have just met with a group of people whose main idea, I'm convinced, is going to be of lasting value to all of us on the left who want a fundamental change in our present social system.'

'And what is this idea?' Cedric asked a little sceptically.

'It is one I think you must already be familiar with, though I was not. It is that the working class in revolt needs the guidance of theory.'

'This is an idea I entirely agree with,' Cedric said. 'And who are these people you've just met?'

'They call themselves professional revolutionaries, and they are confident that a day will come when – with their help and the help of similar groups who are linked together in a single new Internationale – the working-class will be triumphant all over the world and the human race will be united at last.'

'And you have joined this professional organisation?' Cedric asked.

'Yes I have, and I wish you too could join it, but sadly I realise that it would be too strenuous for you. We shall not forget how much we owe to you for the ideas you have given us. But I feel that the best thing you can do, my dearest, is to make your way back now to Dorothy's "safe house". I know she will be happy to have you staying with her. And don't think I'm saying goodbye to you for ever. I'm hopeful that before too long I'll somehow manage to meet you again.'

She bent forward to kiss him, and tears streamed over both their faces.

The Suspect

six short stories

~ THE WAR WIDOW ~

ONE FINE MARCH morning seventy-year-old Trevor Halford was returning along a Southsea street from the usual daily walk he took down to the sea front, when he saw for the first time the new proprietor of the small *Harbour View* hotel. She was standing just behind her garden gate, and he came to a stop and said good-morning to her. She moved up to the gate. She was a handsome woman, in her late thirties perhaps, with dark red hair.

He said, 'May I ask if you are the new proprietor here?'

'You may, and I am,' she answered, giving him a nice smile. 'I think I've seen you passing by more than once before now, haven't I?'

'I daresay you have. This is my favourite route down to the sea. Each morning since I retired I have liked to make my bow to the Solent on my right hand and to Spithead on my left.'

She laughed. 'Are you an ex-naval man?'

'No, I'm an ex-Chartered Accountant from London. I wanted to retire to the South Coast somewhere, and I suppose what caused me to choose Portsmouth was that I had happy childhood memories of seaside summer holidays here.'

'On Portsmouth beach just outside the naval base?!' she asked with smiling irony.

'Of course not.' He laughed. 'You wouldn't describe where we are at this moment as "just outside" the naval base, would you?'

'No, I wouldn't,' she admitted, 'we're really Southsea residents even though we're under Portsmouth City Council.' Her tone changed. 'Before the War I lived in Southsea with my husband John who was in the navy. His ship was based nearby at Portsmouth. He went down with the ship when it was torpedoed by a German submarine soon after the War really began.' She paused, then added, 'A surviving shipmate and friend of his is working with me here in my hotel.'

Trevor, not knowing what to say to her about this, found himself telling her, 'I am living with my wife still, but she is dying of kidney disease.'

'I'm sorry to hear that.'

'I had better return to her now or she may begin to wonder what's happened to me. I hope you and I will see each other again soon.'

'I'm sure we shall,' she said.

While he was walking back to his house after leaving her he was surprised to realise how much he had told her about himself at this their first meeting, and how much she had told him about herself. It was as though each had felt a special need to confide in the other.

He did not mention to his wife Olwyn that he had met the new proprietor of *Harbour View* hotel. He knew she would have been upset if he had mentioned it. As her illness advanced she increasingly suspected him of at least flirting, if nothing worse, with other women, and her suspicions were partly justified, though he never went all the way with any other woman.

He had been very much in love with her when he had married her. She had been eighteen then and he had been twenty-six. They first met at a well-known firm of Chartered Accountants where he earned a good salary and expected to become a partner before long. She worked as a secretary to one of the older partners in the firm. She was in love with Trevor, and the thought that he would be able to provide her and any children they might have with a reasonably high standard of living made him additionally attractive to her.

Their marriage was a success, and although almost from the start he had an eye for other women she never felt the slightest jealousy, being completely sure of his faithfulness to her. They had two children and wanted more, but before long it was necessary for her to have her ovaries removed and she could never become pregnant again. A difference of opinion arose between them when the children reached secondary school age after leaving kindergarten and after they had attended a non-boarding private Preparatory School. They agreed that the elder, Anna, should go to the local Girls' High School. He, however, was keen that the younger, Owen, should go to the 'Public' boarding school for boys which he himself had been educated at before he went on to the University. He argued that if two young candidates of more or less equal ability, one of them from a 'Public' school and the other not, applied for the same job, the one who was not would be much less likely to get the job, unfair though this might be. He convinced her, and she gave way to him. Her main objection had been religious. She was a strict Nonconformist, a Congregationalist, and she would have preferred to send Owen to a boarding school for the sons of well-to-do Congregationalists rather than to a Church of England 'Public' school. Luckily religion caused no other dissension between them, because while she was very much in earnest about her Congregrationalism he remained a tolerant agnostic whose conventional Anglicanism presented no obstacle to his agreeing that she should take their daughter and their son to chapel on Sundays in the holidays.

The first really serious difference between them came during the First World War. Suddenly in the third year of the War he decided to join up, although he was over the age at which he would have been conscripted. She felt he would not have done it if he had genuinely loved her or their children. He must have reached the critical age at which, some say, men feel that their last chance has come to make a clean break with a disappointing past. He also upset his partners in the firm of Chartered Accountants, who thought he was being inconsiderate and who resented the prospect of having to take him back into the firm if he returned from the War.

He did return, miraculously as it seemed to him, and his happiness at seeing Olwyn and their children again was so evident that she knew he'd always loved her and them. He had had his middle-aged fling, and now he was hers once more. He was still wearing his army officer's uniform when he arrived in the hall of his home where they were waiting for him. He had not yet taken off his brown leather belt when he hugged and kissed her and when he kissed the children. They saw the revolver holster attached to the belt and he allowed them to open the holster and take out the heavy revolver. He had removed the large blunt-headed bullets from its rotatable chambers, but a year later Owen was to find the bullets and the revolver in a cupboard in the spare bedroom, and he showed them to his sister Anna. By that time he had become an antimilitarist at his 'Public' school.

Trevor's Chartered Accountant partners soon forgave him, their forgivenesss being made easier by the fact that the firm, which had not been doing well in his absence, quite quickly recovered after his return.

• • •

THE YEARS PASSED, and Anna married, and Owen after getting a first-class degree in History at Cambridge took a badly paid socially useful job.

Meanwhile Trevor was spending more and more of his free time at the golf club, and Olwyn felt she was being neglected. Also she disliked the type of men that he was becoming friendly with there. Particularly Sandy Long, who was widely known to have brought his mistress into the house where he was living with his wife.

When the Second World War began Owen chose to be conscripted into the London fire service rather than the army, in which he would have been taught how to kill people. Trevor regarded Owen's choice as pacifistic and never quite forgave him for it, though actually Owen was not a pacifist and was more strongly anti-fascist than his father was. Trevor put the fight for King and Country first.

Trevor's daughter Anna, who had a young child and was not conscripted but whose husband was, became his favourite.

•

The proprietress of *Harbour View* invited Trevor into the hotel when he saw her in her front garden for the second time, and she introduced him to her late husband's friend Stanley; but before she did this she had to ask what his name was and Trevor after being introduced to Stanley asked her what hers was.

'My maiden name was Molly Mangan, but I always call myself Val, and so does Stanley.'

'And while we're about it, I may as well ask what your married name is,' Trevor said.

'Noakes,' she said.

'And you might like to know that my surname is Wilton,' Stanley said. He may have felt slightly riled that Val had introduced him to Trevor only by his first name. Stanley's voice was quiet and gentlemanly, and Trevor irrationally guessed (judging by hers perhaps) that the voice of her husband had not been either of these things.

The third time he saw her she was standing at her garden gate, and Stanley did not come out of the hotel to join them.

'I shall not call you Molly, nor shall I call you Val,' he said.

'What will you call me?'

'I shall call you Esmeralda.'

'You are laughing at me.'

'No I'm not. Esmeralda means emerald, and your eyes have the colour of emeralds, and it goes very well with your beautiful red hair.'

She laughed, but he could see that she was pleased.

When he thought on his way home about her eyes he remembered their whites, which had looked protrusive and discoloured. He was fairly sure that they hadn't given this impression the second or the first time he had seen her. Perhaps this third time she had been been drinking too much the night before. It did not lessen her attractiveness for him. He himself was a regular drinker, though in his own opinion he never drank to excess, not even in the difficult final phase of Olwyn's illness.

At Olwyn's funeral, which out of respect for her wishes was held at a local Congregational chapel, he remembered their youth together and he grieved deeply for her. His daughter Anna found a woman to housekeep for him, a Mrs Vachell who was competent enough but had an elderly husband who constantly came to sit in the kitchen and whose evenly and penetratingly droning voice became less and less tolerable to Trevor. After a while Trevor took to spending more and more of his time at *Harbour View* till finally he told Mrs Vachell he no longer needed her services and Esmeralda moved in to take her place, deserting the unlucky Stanley. She sold *Harbour View*, which hadn't been prospering.

Trevor soon discovered that Esmeralda had a 'drink problem', in other words she was an alcoholic to the point of being a dipsomaniac. It was no wonder that she'd not been a success as an hotelier. Yet her problem did not prevent her from cooking meals for him which he found palatable and quite adequate, his appetite for solid food not being as large as it might have been if he himself hadn't been a regular whisky drinker.

Anna came down from her married home in Suffolk for one of her frequent long weekend visits to see how her father was getting on, and this time she was rather anxiously expecting to be introduced to Val (whose pet name of Esmeralda her father had not yet revealed to her). Esmeralda was at least as anxious as Anna about their meeting. Wanting to make a good impression on Anna she had drunk much less than usual. She was able to produce an excellent meal for them all. At the end of the meal he asked her to recite from Shakespeare's 'Famous History of the Life of King Henry VIII', Cardinal Wolsey's speech which ends with the lines, 'Had I but served my God with half the zeal/I served my king, he would not in mine age/Have left me naked to mine enemies.'

Anna was greatly impressed by the verve and the obvious understanding with which Val recited the speech, and in appreciation of it she was moved to clap her hands. Val was very relieved and pleased, and Trevor was delighted. Then he asked her to recite the one other piece she knew by heart – Anna did not guess that she knew only two pieces – Kipling's poem about the Prodigal Son who before coming home again is reduced to working in the stockyards of Chicago. Anna was even more impressed by this. The emotional depth which Val's voice gave it suggested that she must be thinking of something in her own life as she recited it.

On the Monday morning of this weekend Trevor came out of the front door with Anna to see her off.

'Well,' he said, 'and what do you think of my woman?'

Partly because she'd genuinely admired Val's recitations, and still more because she was glad that her father now had someone to look after him, but most of all because she knew that if she'd expressed the least disapproval of Val he would never have forgiven her – she answered, 'I think she's wonderful.'

As she drove home on her longish journey back to Suffolk she increasingly felt that during the whole of the weekend Val had been at pains to appear reliable and likeable, even preparing some very nice sandwiches for her to take with her on her journey. And Anna intuitively – though she hoped she was wrong – suspected that this behaviour was misleading. She had noticed the unhealthy protrusiveness of Val's eyeballs.

It took some while for Trevor to realise that Esmeralda was drinking more than was good for her or him. This was first brought to his attention by the size of the bills he was getting from his wine merchant. However, he knew he could afford it, and he did not protest to her about it. But a time arrived when she became less and less capable of preparing meals for him and he had to prepare them for her.

He succeeded in persuading her to go temporarily into a nursing home where she would be helped to come off drink.

He found he hated being alone in the house at nights and he kept a carving knife by his bedside to deal with any burglar who might break in.

One night Esmeralda decided she'd had enough of the nursing home and she hired a taxi to take her back to Trevor. When he heard the front door bell ring he went downstairs holding his carving knife and opened the door to her. The taxi-driver saw him with the knife and drove off quickly to the nearest police station.

After a by no means short interval a policeman reached the house.

'Come and see the corpse,' Trevor said to him, and took him upstairs to show him Esmeralda in bed.

Esmeralda did not refrain altogether from drinking after she returned to Trevor, though for a while she drank less than before, but not surprisingly she was soon drinking as much as or more than ever. Trevor packed his bag and left her, not telling her where he was going.

He got in touch with Jim Lascombe, a solicitor twenty years his junior who had belonged to a golf club in the London area, of which Trevor was once chosen to be Captain, and Jim had already shown admiration for him before then. Like Esmeralda, Jim had been an alchoholic. He had eventually disgraced himself as a solicitor, but he had become a member of Alcoholics Anonymous and he was now effectively cured. He was living with his two sisters in a small house in a Cotswold town. He kept up a regular correspondence with Trevor, who after leaving Esmeralda phoned to ask if he could come and stay with him; and Jim gladly said he could. Trevor, as he finished his phone call, felt a peculiar misgiving. He remembered how unpredictably embarrassing Jim had formerly been at times, and how once, when early in Trevor's retirement to Southsea he arrived at night by car and couldn't remember Trevor's address, he had called in very drunk at the police station to ask for it. Fortunately he seemed to have been able to disguise his drunken state from the police. But why should this long ago incident cause Trevor the slightest misgiving now?

Trevor took a taxi from the station to Jim's small house, and Jim after introducing him to his sisters led him to a bedroom and mentioned that a weekly payment for it would be helpful. Trevor was very willing to agree to this, but he was totally opposed to what happened three days after his arrival. In the night Jim entered his room and got naked into bed with him. Trevor vigorously shoved him out. Next morning Jim was very apologetic and promised he would never be guilty of such behaviour towards him again.

'You had better not be,' Trevor said, and his life with Jim and with Jim's sisters continued, but not quite as before. He realised now that Jim was a gerontophile and could have felt similarly towards him when both of them were twenty years younger and when Trevor was totally unaware that Jim's admiration for him was gerontophilic. From now on Jim's feelings would have to return to being strictly platonic, though even his occasional platonic manifestations of admiration in the days that followed were repellent to Trevor.

Esmeralda soon found Trevor's absence unbearable, and her friend Mavis from the wine merchant's happened to look in one day and discovered that she was lying unconscious on the floor of the sitting-room, and there was a large hole burnt in the carpet just beside her face. She had been smoking a cigarette and it was lucky that she hadn't been burnt to death. Mavis phoned Dr Jenkins, who arrived and gave orders that Mrs Noakes should be taken to the local mental hospital.

After three days at the hospital Esmeralda indignantly demanded that she should be discharged. As they had no right to keep her there against her will they let her go, though not before a psychiatrist at the hospital suggested to her that it might be a good thing for her to get in touch soon with Alcoholics Anonymous.

She took the advice and became a member of this useful organisation. She had now one supreme aim in life – to get Trevor back. But she did not know where he was, and neither Anna nor Owen who both did know would admit to her that they did. She employed a local girl to keep the house tidy, and she waited patiently though not unhopefully for Trevor's return. Something told her that he would become increasingly dissatisfied with living away from her.

And she was right. Anna and Owen were much dismayed when she told them triumphantly that he had written her a letter. She ironically gave them his address which they had said they did not know. She answered his letter, and two days later she hired a taxi and was driven expensively to Lascombe's small house in the Cotswolds. While the taxi-driver waited, a scene of bitter hostility took place inside the house between Jim and Esmeralda, until Trevor appeared from his bedroom with his bag packed and, after thanking Jim and Jim's sisters for their hospitality, walked behind her out of the front door. No one waved goodbye to them from the door.

When she had got him back to the house a new supreme aim was soon formed in her mind. She would turn him against Anna as well as against Owen and against both their spouses, and then she would persuade him to marry her and would inherit most of his property. She was quite frank about trying to get him to marry her. Upstairs one evening in front of Anna and Owen she had smilingly pleaded with him, raising both her arms in supplication towards him, to decide soon to make her an honest woman by marrying her. They were partly reassured by knowing that she had failed to lure him into a double-bed she had recently bought, though several roguish remarks such as 'naughty, naughty' which on other occasions she had made to him in front of them, and his embarrassing chuckles in response, left them in no doubt that some kind of sexual happenings were going on between them. But their fears that she might eventually gain complete control over him were put at rest by something Owen witnessed as Trevor was on his way to bed one night.

Esmeralda was a Catholic (not a practising one) and she had positioned an almost life-size painted plaster bust of the Virgin Mary on the surface of a chest-of-drawers in the short passageway between her bedroom and his. Trevor who was growing bald had taken to keeping the back of his head warm during the daytime by wearing a dark blue beret. Owen saw him remove this and then, just before reaching the door of his bedroom, clap it on to the painted Virgin's head. Anna had evidence too that Esmeralda herself had given up hope of getting a promise of marriage from Trevor. Once Esmeralda when she was alone with Anna in the dining-room said to her, 'A girl should learn to play her cards better than I did.' There was an apparent light-heartedness in her tone, although she obviously felt that if she had been able to prevent herself from drinking to excess she could have brought him round to promising he would marry her. She had a good store of amusingly cynical phrases which she used on occasions of varying seriousness. Describing to Owen how an elderly man, whose intentions according to her turned out to be innocent, invited her into his house one day, she said, 'and I thought to myself, rough check, what's he after?' Among other favourite phrases of hers were, 'If rape is inevitable, relax and enjoy it,' and 'Press on regardless.' Nevertheless, though using such phrases in conversation with Anna and Owen and with their spouses, she was plotting all the while to turn Trevor against each one of them, and she very nearly succeeded.

She turned him first against Owen's wife Rosa, who in her hearing had once incautiously remarked that an antique bureau in the drawing-room might be quite valuable. Esmeralda reported this to Trevor who immediately suspected, as she had calculated he would, that Rosa was eager to possess the bureau after he died. He told Owen that on his next visit here he was not to bring Rosa with him. And his displeasure with Owen himself, which already existed because of what Trevor incorrectly regarded as Owen's pacifism, was compounded by his old-fashioned view that a husband should at least be able to keep his own wife in order. The next success Esmeralda achieved was in turning him against Anna's husband Vincent, a doctor, who asked Esmeralda if she had yet tried to persuade Trevor that it might be good for him if he could agree to reduce the amount of wine and spirits he was at present drinking. Vincent was aware that Esmeralda was now a member of Alcoholics Anonymous and he felt she would be glad to know she had his medical support if she was trying to do this. Trevor was furious when she reported Vincent's talk with her, and he told Anna before the day came for her to go back home with Vincent that he never wanted to see Vincent again.

'Oh but Daddy,' Anna said in great distress, 'he did not mean any harm, he just wanted to be helpful.'

Suddenly a look of remorse came over his face because of the distress he saw he had caused her. She was his favourite child and so long as she approved of his relationship with Esmeralda he would never let anyone turn him against her. But though he did not object when Anna on one of her future visits to Southsea brought Vincent with her again, Trevor found it difficult to conceal his continuing dislike of him. Owen on the other hand did not attempt to make Trevor believe the truth that when Rosa had said the bureau might be valuable she had spoken in all innocence and without any expectation of inheriting it. Vincent's remark to Esmeralda about Trevor's drinking had been rather more justly resented by Trevor than Rosa's remark about the bureau had been, yet Owen felt that trying to convince Trevor of Rosa's innocence would only intensify his displeasure with Owen himself. And Rosa's own pride would not have allowed her to try to accompany Owen to his father's house again in any case.

Trevor's health had not been improved by his disturbing adventures after he had packed his bag and walked out on Esmeralda. Within two years of his return to her he was increasingly complaining of swollen ankles, which he feared might be due to heart disease. She insisted he should see a doctor, but not Dr Jenkins who had sent her to the mental hospital. Dr Alverton came instead. He gave Trevor a thorough examination, and confirmed Trevor's unprofessional diagnosis of heart disease.

'Can it be cured?' Trevor asked.

'It can be treated,' Dr Alverton evasively answered.

'I don't want that,' Trevor said, and so firmly that Dr Alverton did not try to persuade him to change his mind.

The doctor left the house and Trevor was alone again in the south sitting-room with Esmeralda.

'I think this demands a double whisky and a cigar,' he said to her.

Several days later, prompted by her, he began to think about making changes in her favour to his will. He phoned the Portsmouth solicitor who had drawn up a will for him soon after he had retired to Southsea.

The solicitor arrived in the afternoon to see him, and her, and to discuss with them the details of the changes he wanted. She had to accept with a good grace Trevor's decision that not she but Anna should inherit the house and should be appointed together with the solicitor as executors of his will.

When Anna next came down to visit him he told her about his heart trouble, and he also told Owen who visited him soon afterwards.

At Christmas time each of them had a phone call from Esmeralda to say that their father was very ill and that they should come at once.

Owen arrived first and found his father already unconscious and breathing heavily as he lay on a couch in the south sitting-room. He was still breathing heavily and unconsciously when Anna arrived. But suddenly as she looked at him his breathing stopped. She bent down over him.

• • •

'DADDY!' SHE SAID. She stood up again, and she wept.

Owen standing beside her did not weep, though he grieved greatly for him.

He said, 'We must get a doctor to certify that he is dead.'

As soon as he had walked out of the room to phone Dr Alverton, Esmeralda came into it.

She showed little emotion. Anna, who had been appointed by her father in his will as an executor together with his Portsmouth solicitor, knew that though it made quite handsome financial provision for Esmeralda it did not bequeath the house to her, which was what she had probably above all been hoping for. Her showing so little grief at Trevor's death could well be due, Anna guessed, to disappointment.

But Anna was wrong. It was in fact due to sheer emotional exhaustion after the weeks during which at night as well as in the daytime she had been attending with a minimal amount of sleep or respite to the needs of the dying man. He wanted no one else to attend to him, though he was sadly aware of the strain he was causing her and he urged her to help him put an end to himself. 'Don't keep me here any longer, Esmeralda,' he said, which she understood to mean he wanted her to leave his sleeping pills within his reach so that he could take an overdose. She was tempted to do this as an act of mercy, but she dared not.

Owen was quite a time out of the room phoning Dr Alderton. When he came back he reported that Alderton who had known that his patient would die soon and not liking to be called out at night had asked angrily, 'Can't you tell whether he's dead or not?' Owen answered that he thought it was the usual thing for a family doctor to come on these occasions, and Alderton then relented and would soon be here.

Alderton very briefly examined the pyjamaed body of Trevor, which was covered almost up to the shoulders with bed-clothes, and said, 'Poor old boy, poor old boy.' There was kindness and penitence in his voice.

Next morning Esmeralda got in touch with a woman she had met in one of the local pubs who now and again earned a pound or two by 'laying out' the bodies of the dead. She arrived that day and Esmeralda fortified her in her task by providing her with a large glass mug of stout.

Two days later the coffin and the undertaker, quite an old man himself, arrived, and after finishing his work alone on the corpse in the south sitting-room he came into the drawing-room to speak to Owen and Anna with tears in his eyes which seemed so genuine that both of them were fully convinced that these had not been produced with the help of an onion or glycerine.

At the funeral service in the Anglican church and at the burial afterwards in the churchyard, Esmeralda was present together with Anna and Owen. But when the ceremony was over and they all three of them went back to the house, she told Anna and Owen she had decided to have a short holiday away from it all in a top class London hotel. They willingly acquiesced, though without saying so they hoped for her sake that she wouldn't squander too much of the money their father had left her. The three of them were agreed that she should continue living in the house when Anna and Owen, who were glad of a few free days now to begin to sort out a mass of their father's papers, had to return home, Owen to his job and Anna to her husband.

Emeralda was hoping to be allowed by Anna and Owen to live permanently in this house she loved and formerly shared with Trevor, and she had thoughts of running it as a home for old men.

She expected that Anna, though having a right to take over the house, would prefer to stay on in her own more modern Suffolk one, and that Owen would choose to remain in London near to the head office of the charitable organisation he had dedicated his life to. Esmeralda was right about Owen's intentions, but wrong about Anna's. Anna wanted to return to the house, mainly because her doctor husband was keen to retire early and in good health and to get far away from his patients who might still wish to consult him.

Anna drove down to Southsea with considerable anxiety to break the news of her intentions to Esmeralda.

'And what do you think is going to happen to me?' Esmeralda asked bitterly.

'My father did leave you quite a large sum of money,' Anna said diffidently.

'But not a house.'

'I sympathise with you very much. I don't know what I would do if I were in your place. Perhaps I would look for some other elderly man I could help.'

Anna spent the night in the house, but she took the precaution of fixing the top of a chair tightly beneath the door-handle of her bedroom door.

Owen also came down to see Esmeralda. He had to listen to her complaints against Anna, and though alarmed by her extreme bitterness he couldn't prevent himself from feeling rather disloyally relieved that she did not blame him at all.

Anna several days later drove down to see Owen in London and to tell him that she wanted to compensate for her father's leaving less money to him than to her in his will. She would even up the difference by writing him a cheque now. He thanked her very much. She stayed the night in his flat and next day she drove down to Southsea to visit Esmeralda a second time and to assure her that she need not be in any hurry to move out of the house. Anna explained that she herself and her husband had many things still to do before they would be ready to leave their present home.

Esmeralda, before Anna started on her drive back to Suffolk that same day, astoundingly said to her, 'When Owen came down to see me not long ago he told me the best thing I could do now would be to find another old man with a house I could live in. He did not know how near death he was at that moment.' Was Esmeralda only pretending to have forgotten that it was Anna not Owen who had made that death-deserving suggestion?

At last Anna and her husband were ready to move from Suffolk to the house in Southsea. She wrote to Esmeralda several weeks beforehand, giving her plenty of time to make her own move to wherever she had arranged to go. Anna was not altogether surprised to get no answer from her. But when Anna and her husband arrived at their Southsea house they found that Esmeralda had stripped it bare of many of its furnishings – carpets and curtains and armchairs, and even early photographs of Anna's father and mother.

Anna was very angry and got in touch with the Portsmouth solicitor who had drawn up her father's will. Within a month he managed to persuade Esmeralda to return much but not all that she had taken. He did not press her too hard: he may have thought he had a duty to Trevor to protect her from the hostility of his children.

And then Anna had a letter from Esmeralda which she would not be able to forget for the rest of her life.

•

Esmeralda's letter began by admitting that she ought not to have removed from the house those things she was not entitled by Trevor's will to have, but she had acted under great provocation from Anna. She accused Anna of a lack of human sympathy. Couldn't Anna imagine what it had been like for a young wife to lose a husband, also young, in the war? It was this loss that had caused Esmeralda to take to drink, and it was drink that had caused her to 'look for an old man whose house she could live in.' Anna might have behaved more reputably if she had lost her husband, but would she then have thought less unkindly of women who, like Esmeralda, were not gifted with her own moral strength? And had she ever realised that some of the faults of her own father might have been due to his war experiences? Esmeralda's letter, which throughout was written in the kind of English then regarded as 'educated' (that's to say its 'grammar' and its punctuation were correct), was full of vigour and of literary echoes, and it ended with a meaningful quotation from Pope:

'To err is human, to forgive divine.'

Anna did forgive her, but felt it would seem arrogant if she wrote to tell her so. She never wrote to her.

•

A few months later Esmeralda wrote Anna a short letter saying, 'I am now living with George.'

•

It was clear that Esmeralda had forgiven Anna.

~ IMAGINATIVE MEN & WOMEN ~

EARLY ONE FINE autumnal Saturday afternoon, during the Second World War, Dr Andrew Elford was waiting for the ferry-boat which would take him across from the south to the north side of the estuary. Almost always, whatever the time of year might be, the south side was very windy, and today he was looking forward both to meeting old friends living on the north side and to escaping into the remarkably milder climate that prevailed there. Quite possibly the northern weather now might still be warm enough for them and him to sit and talk and eat together out-of-doors.

•

Andrew's wait for the ferry-boat was much longer than he had expected. He had arrived too soon at the small pier on the south side, probably because of an over-eagerness to reach what he hoped to be the calmer north. He was deterred from feeling irritably restive, however, by remembering that the force of the wind which was buffeting him here on the pier was as nothing compared with its violence when he had to bicycle against it in a rain-proof suit to visit his patients.

•

At last a swirling column of thick black smoke mounting into the clean blustery air told him that the high-funnelled antiquated ferry-boat was making its way back from the far side towards him as he stood waiting.

•

On its deck during its return to the northern pier he was hardly conscious at all of the wind which was blowing more strongly than ever. Then, after he had landed, and had left the pier behind him, the word 'paradise' rose into his mind at his first glimpse – beyond trees that had several Cedars of Lebanon among them – of the house his friends Sid and Gladys Palmer lived in.

He found them digging in their garden. They didn't believe in possessing a telephone, so he had not been able to let them know in advance of his decision to visit them today. They were surprised to see him, but there could be no doubt about the complete genuineness of their delight that he had come.

'But why hasn't Mary come with you?' Gladys asked.

'Mary would very much have liked to come,' Andrew said, 'but all three of the children have got colds and one of us parents had to stay with them. Mary insisted that I had been working too hard during the week and it would do no harm if I were to ask Dr Ragnell, my senior partner in our practice, to take over from me this weekend for a change. So here I am on my own.' Then he added with a grin, 'And, anyway, looking after the children is her official war work: if it weren't for them she would have been conscripted into the army.'

'But what about yourself?' Gladys asked him with concern. 'Mightn't you still get conscripted?'

'Well, it could happen,' Andrew admitted. 'I have been thinking of myself as being a little too old to be called up now, just as I was a little too young to be called up in the First War. But if there were heavy losses among younger doctors who have been conscripted I think I would be quite likely to be taken – and I would go willingly enough because I believe that the Nazis are a far deadlier menace to the human race than the Kaiser's Germany ever was. This present war is very different from the First.'

Andrew, luckily, realised almost instantly that his remark about the difference between the two wars might get him into the kind of fruitlessly obstinate argument with Sid that he especially wanted to avoid. He quickly said to Sid, 'But I think I remember your telling me that in the First War no one seemed to regard you as too old to enlist, though you must have been at least as old then as I am now.'

'How right you are,' Sid said. 'I was employed as an assistant gardener by an Anglican Rector who came of a very aristocratic family, and he was proud to see me go. I fancy he would have been even prouder if I'd been killed and he'd been able to put up a bronze plaque in his church to my memory.' Sid laughed, and added, 'But things didn't work out like that at all. I was captured by the enemy only a day or two after we reached the front.'

'You sound as though you weren't too sorry about it?'

'I wasn't. I let them know I'd been a gardener in civil life, and they allowed me to do a little work for a German farmer some way behind their lines, under military guard of course.'

Grinning, Andrew quoted,

> *and one, to use the word of 'ypocrites*
> *'ad the misfortoon to be took by Fritz.*

'I like that,' Sid said.

'It comes from a poem written by our best war poet.'

But Sid showed no sign of caring who wrote the poem. There was something important to him that he wanted to let Andrew know. 'It is a strange thing,' he said, 'that when I was a prisoner of war on a German farm I first became keen on agriculture.'

'Would you have liked to stay on after the war and become a farmer in Germany?'

'Good Lord, no.' Sid laughed loudly.

'That could be taken to mean you don't like Germans.'

'I liked them – those I got to know – very much,' Sid said forcefully. 'Including my military guard. But this home here is where I want to live. With Gladys of course. And to dig our garden.'

She gave Andrew an interested look; and the thought came to him, as it had never done before, that she might agree with those early socialists who believed in 'free love'.

He quickly got back to the subject of nationalities by saying, 'I knew a man who had been a German prisoner of war in this country and who chose to stay on here. One summer Mary and I were having a fortnight's holiday together in the south of England. We'd found a very pleasant house which had only one disadvantage: the owner who rented it to us, and was himself going away for a holiday, kept chickens in a wire enclosure at the end of his garden, and he asked us to do something for them, give them water or grain – I can't remember exactly what.'

Sid commented with affable sarcasm, 'You must have enjoyed that.'

'The owner assured us we could get help from his neighbour, the German prisoner who had stayed on, if we had any trouble with the chickens.'

'And I suppose you did,' Gladys guessed from Andrew's tone of voice.

'Yes,' he said. 'We were horrified to see that one of the chickens was being mercilessly attacked by the others who were viciously pecking its neck. "They'll kill it," Mary said.'

'The German ex-prisoner, a very friendly man, came along and lifted up the attacked chicken in his arms and took it away with him. Two or three days later he brought it back and dropped it in among the others, who accepted it without the least hostility. He explained that it had been suffering from something like what might be called a cold in the nose, and that he'd been able to cure this.'

•

'And what moral do you expect us to draw from your holiday story?' a man's voice suddenly and a little truculently asked. He was Clem Marsden, a friend of the Palmers, living with his wife Alice in a small nearby cottage. Andrew, who had met him once before, said amicably, 'I don't know of any moral I would draw from it, though perhaps it does suggest to me that if I had the time to spare I might like to take up the study of the behaviour of birds in general.'

'You could *make* the time, if you wanted to,' Marsden said almost severely.

Gladys changed the subject for them by saying, 'I think it might be a good idea for all of us now to have tea.'

Andrew had learnt from his middle-class (but politically very left-wing) wife Mary that for the middle class 'to have tea' meant having, between four and half-past in the afternoon a cup of tea, and a slice of cake, or even cucumber sandwiches, whereas for the great majority of the British population it was the main meal of the day, and was usually eaten between six and half-past.

Didn't this mean, Andrew half-humorously asked himself, that Sid and Gladys whose origins were certainly working-class had become bourgeoisified? And that he had become so too, his parents having been petty-bourgeois shopkeepers whose tea was at six thirty? Yes, but at least in their politics both he and Sid, and Gladys and bourgeois-born Mary, were wholeheartedly on the side of the exploited working class. However, what did or could they do politically now?

'I've brought some cherry cake,' Andrew said, intending not to tell them till after they'd eaten it that the cherries were really bits of beetroot.

'That's very sweet of you,' Gladys told him, 'or perhaps I should say it's very sweet of Mary who I daresay was the one who actually made the cake.'

'Yes, she did,' Andrew admitted.

'Clem and Alice are also kindly contributing,' Gladys went on, 'and now I think the time has come for us to fetch out the garden chairs and table from the garden shed; though when I say us I really mean all you, not including me, because I shall be bringing out from the house the actual tea – that's to say the hot liquid in a teapot – together with the milk.'

Soon after they had begun their tea-meal, Clem suddenly said, 'It is almost difficult to believe we are in the middle of a deadly war.'

'It may not go on for very much longer,' Sid said.

'More likely it will never stop,' Clem said, 'or not until most of the human race have succeeded in exterminating themselves.'

'Why is he so bitterly pessimistic?' Gladys asked his wife Alice.

'I may get into trouble with him for telling you what I think might partly account for it.' She turned to her husband and said, 'You have several times described to me how on one occasion you saw men blown to "bits of meat" by an exploding shell. I think the incident preyed on your mind.'

'Whose minds wouldn't it have preyed on, except those of – to quote the poet I'm told is Andrew's favourite war poet – "dullards whom no cannon stuns." '

Neither Andrew nor Sid nor Gladys asked Alice or Clem why this one horrible incident that preyed on his mind had convinced him that the present war would go on till most of the human race were exterminated by it.

•

Dr Andrew had an alarmed suspicion that Clem might be on the verge of a serious mental breakdown,

Ironically, Andrew did not remember that the war poet greatly admired by him and perfectly sane, Wilfred Owen, seemed in a poem entitled 'The End' to take an even more pessimistic view than Clem did.

But the old-time socialist Sid argued, as the meal went on, that in the not too distant future most of the human race would have learnt at last that wars were of no benefit to them, and there would then be no more wars.

Andrew, however, said, 'Although I agree with you that wars will ultimately be abolished I am convinced there will have to be a long and bitter struggle before this.'

•

He became aware, as they all sat comfortably enough around the garden table, that though the air remained warm it was growing darker. He would soon have to leave if he was to be in time to catch the last ferry to the south. Suddenly they all heard the throbbing drone of aircraft flying in formation high overhead, and then far to the north soon afterwards there were loud bright explosions while criss-crossing searchlights scissored the sky.

'They are bombing the shipyards,' Sid said. 'They are not interested in small fry like us living here.'

'We've sometimes heard those explosions and seen those search-lights from where we live,' Andrew said. 'They seemed very distant. We ourselves are within three miles of a large chemical factory which in spite of its conspicuously high chimneys appears to be immune from attack. There are rumours that a similar factory in Germany is owned by the same powerful company and is equally immune.'

'Did you create the rumours, by any chance?' Clem bluntly asked.

'Well, perhaps I did contribute to them,' Andrew frankly said.

'Quite rightly,' Sid said vigorously. 'They are obviously true.'

When Andrew arrived home that evening he gave Mary an account of the talk at the tea party, and she was particularly interested to hear of Sid's vigorous assertion of belief in the 'rumour' that explained why the chemical factory remained unbombed.

But also she wondered whether its being a *chemical* factory was particularly repulsive to him.

She was wrong about this.

•

Sid had no objection to chemicals so long as they benefited agriculture without harming either the farm-workers who had to use them or the surrounding country and the people who lived there – 'the environment', as it was officially called, to Sid's distaste.

•

Sid thought often about workers on the land. He thought, as he dug in his garden, about those working in other countries besides Britain, women as well as men. His mind pictured women in the flooded paddy fields stooping to implant the rice-plants beneath the shallow water which covered their bare feet, and he knew that this bareness could cause disease, and he thought of the poverty which prevented the women from providing themselves with protective high boots. He thought of Africa and of farmers there who were forced to abandon their farming by wars that the rivalry of outside Powers had caused, and he thought of the starving African children with swollen bellies.

•

He thought too of England in the past, and he felt an affinity with Gerrard Winstanley, 'the Digger', who during the period of the Commonwealth had insisted that all the land belonged to the whole people of England. Sid imagined Winstanley's setting out one Sunday morning with a few followers to dig the waste land on St George's Hill in Surrey and to begin the establishment of a community there, and he vividly saw their brutal ejection a fortnight later by Cromwell's soldiers.

•

But of land-workers in twentieth-century countries he thought mostly about those rebelling in South America. His mind saw the death-squads in action and horrifically murdered bodies flung into roadside ditches. Then his mind foresaw at last a decisive battle won in a South American country by rebel peasants who thereafter ceased to be peasants and became free. And Sid dreamed as he dug in his garden that the same thing, perhaps all the sooner because of their example, would happen in every country where there were peasants still, and that the transition would be less murderous when land-owners understood how profitably they could exploit 'free' waged labourers.

• • •

Sid dreamed further of laws that would curb and finally put an end to such exploitation and would bring about the common ownership of all the land by all the people. He dreamed of richly green fields and of preserved hedges and of cared-for woodlands. He dreamed of new agricultural machines which without polluting the air or the soil would make work far easier for the farm workers who operated them. He never doubted, and Gladys agreed with him, that wars would come and wars would go, but the cultivation of the earth would continue and would save the human race from self-extinction.

•

Mary often daydreamed of a future in which all discrimination against women was brought to an end. When her three children were grown up and had left home she felt she had the time and the duty to do something to help the cause of women's 'liberation'. She found several local women who were willing to co-operate with her in arranging public meetings. Their heroine was Mary Wollstonecraft, who wrote *A Vindication of the Rights of Woman*.

Andrew was entirely in favour of Mary's work, but he thought he'd better not show this, because some patients if he did might suspect him of caring a bit less for them than for politics.

•

And what about Clem Marsden? Did he still say wars would go on till most humans were extinct? Yes, but his wife found out he was day-dreaming of being in a space vehicle travelling far faster than light and arriving outside the supposedly finite 'universe' at a place where life existed in a physical form much less disadvantaged than the human body, and where he would be happier than he could ever have been on the earth.

~ THE SERIAL DREAMER ~

EDWIN ARCOTT after his bereavement was often asked out for an evening meal by his married friends Robert and Jean Kelly, or Albert and Phyllis Turner, or Harry and Jessy Frazer. It was during an evening at the house of Robert and Jean that the talk got on to the subject of dreams. Albert and Phyllis were also there, and Albert had become involved in a political argument with Robert, who had maintained that if the Labour Party under its new leadership were to win the next election it might be even worse than the present Tory Government.

'So on the whole you would prefer to see the Tories win, would you?' Albert asked.

'I never suggested anything of the sort,' Robert said.

'But if you go around telling people who have usually voted Labour that the present leader of the Labour Party is more Tory than some of the Tories,' Albert said quite heatedly, 'you are helping to disillusion possible Labour voters.'

'I'm not prepared to let the interests of any political party prevent me from telling the truth,' Robert said.

Edwin, feeling that this argument between his two friends was not going to get anywhere, asked them, 'Do either of you ever have political dreams?'

Each of them said he didn't. 'Why do you ask?' Albert said.

'Because as far as I can remember I had none during all my years of political work in the Communist Party,' Edwin said, 'and I wanted to know whether you who have strong political feelings have been as politically dreamless as I was.'

'Did you have dreams of any kind?' Phyllis asked.

'Oh yes. I had dreams of personal power, for instance.'

'That sounds political,' she said.

'They weren't political at all. I several times dreamt with complete conviction that I could fly round a room as though I was swimming.'

'I used to have a very similar dream,' Robert said. 'I would stand on one foot and give a little push and in an instant I would be up in the air flying with an easy breast-stroke towards the ceiling. Then I would say to all the people who were suddenly standing below me and gazing at me with admiring amazement, "You see, it's perfectly simple." '

'Do you still have this dream sometimes?' Edwin asked.

'No, I don't,' Robert said.

'Nor do I,' Edwin said, 'but I've recently dreamed that I have the power to enter a room invisibly and intangibly.'

'No doubt you were able to watch some interesting happenings,' Albert said with a meaningful grin.

'Yes,' Edwin said, 'but they were not of the kind you seem to be hinting at. Two nights ago I dreamt I was able to enter the room which is shown in a large engraving you may have noticed hanging on the wall over my drawing-room mantelpiece. But I won't start telling you what I saw inside the room in the engraving. That would take too long.'

He had successfully diverted Albert and Robert from their political argument, and they were soon arguing about the merits of a film they had both of them seen on television. Edwin, who'd also seen it, was able to contribute to the argument.

• • •

The room shown in the engraving had two windows, large, each giving a clear view of what was outside the house, the left-hand one showing several near-by dismal square-looking buildings and a square-looking church, the right-hand one showing a harbour and a big sailing ship towards which three men under the direction of a fourth were conveying provisions for a long voyage – so Edwin guessed – the foremost of them carrying a bulging sack on his bowed back, the second of them trundling a barrel, the third straining to lift up an evidently weighty unidentifiable flat object from the ground. And beyond the harbour the arches of a bridge were visible. The sky above this was threateningly dark.

Inside the room the two large elaborately gilt-framed paintings hanging from the wall were significant. In the lower one a white-hatted white-bearded stern-looking man was sitting at a table while the first of three younger men, all of them having doffed their hats, was pouring coins from his hand on to the table; and as Edwin happened to be familar with the parable of the talents in the Gospel of St Matthew, he knew that the stern-looking man was a master who before travelling into a far country had called his servants together and had delivered to them his goods, and to one he gave five talents, to another he gave two and to the third he gave one talent – to each according to his ability. Then the first servant went and traded with his five talents and made five additional talents, while the servant with two made an additional two, but the servant with only one talent dug a hole and hid his lord's money. When the lord returned from his journey he praised the two servants who had made profits, calling them good and faithful and promising them that, as they had been faithful over a few things, he would promote them to be rulers over many things. But he called the servant who had buried his talent wicked and slothful, telling him that his talent would be taken from him and given to the servant who already had ten talents, and that he ought to have put the money to the exchangers so that his lord when returning would have received his own money with usury. Finally he gave orders that the unprofitable servant should be cast into outer darkness where there would be weeping and gnashing of teeth.

The gilt-framed painting higher up on the wall showed a peasant sowing seed by hand, and Edwin realised that this was intended to illustrate the parable of the sower some of whose seed fell by the way-side and was devoured by birds, some fell on stony places where there was little earth and springing up prematurely was scorched by the sun, some fell among thorns which grew up and choked it, but other seed fell into good ground where it brought forth fruit, an hundredfold, sixtyfold, thirtyfold. The relevance of this to the general message of the engraving – that a man should be profitably enterprising in life – was perhaps a little unclear. Ought the sower to have been been more careful about where he scattered his seed? Or did the painter mean that a man should aim to be the good ground on which some of the seed falls?

There was no ambiguity about the message that the statue of Dick Whittington high up at the back of the room, on top of a tall two-doored eighteenth-century cupboard with a bureau beneath it, was intended to give us. According to legend he was a poor boy who having failed in his ambition to become rich in London went out into the country with his cat, but there before he had walked far he heard bells which seemed to ring out the words, 'Turn again Whittington, Lord Mayor of London.' And he did turn, with his cat, and he became three times Lord Mayor of London, besides becoming extremely rich.

At each end of the base of the statue was a beehive carved in stone, emphasising the virtue of getting busy, and against the wall above the window that looked out on to the harbour there was a clock, on one side of which a cock was carved and on the other an owl. Clearly its message was that time and tide wait for no man.

There were six living human beings and three living animals, two cats and a dog, in the room. The tallest figure here was a man aged perhaps forty, elegantly dressed in a long many-buttoned white silk waistcoat, a white cravat, a black jacket with lacy frills at the wrists, and dark velvet-seeming breeches fastened round his knees. He was presumably the father of the children he was saying goodbye to before departing on an enterprise abroad which would not be without its risks.

There were two little girls aged approximately six and four and a schoolboy aged eleven or twelve. The elder of the little girls was standing on a chair and reaching up an arm to his shoulder, hoping perhaps that he would lift her up and kiss her; but he not being in the mood for such an uninhibited expression of his feelings, merely looked down wistfully at her, while the schoolboy wearing a frilled open-necked jacket was holding out a large book towards him and pointing a finger at something in the text – some biblical verse appropriate to the occasion of his coming voyage, it might be. The younger girl, however, was teasing a kitten and seemed quite uninterested in her father's imminent departure. His wife, the children's mother, was sitting white-bonneted at a table where she had been busy with her needlework when her husband had entered the room to tell them all that the time had come for him to leave them. Her opened hand was letting fall to the floor a piece of material she had been sewing. Her scissors were lying on the table next to a large basket filled with other material, and on the window sill there was a bird-cage inside which a canary (blinded?) was singing with its beak wide open.

The father's valet, who was the only other man in the room, stood near the door, holding his master's cloak draped over his arm. He wore sheenless stockings and a black tail-coat, and his hair unlike his master's (which might have been a wig) was quite black. He was a young man seeing sympathetically the apparent nonchalance of the father, whose shinily stockinged legs were crossed so that the tip of the toe of one of his brightly buckled shoes touched the carpeted floor, and as he looked down into the face of his elder daughter his left hand dangled limply from the frilled wrist of his jacket.

The only dog in the room was looking up doubtfully at the unheeding valet, unsure whether he was going to be taken for a walk or left behind. But at the feet of the wife a large cat in the forefront of the engraving stared directly out of it in a hostile way as if detecting somehow the invisible and intangible presence of Edwin.

• • •

Edwin made a guess that this engraving had been published at the beginning of the nineteenth century when the British fleet was superior to the French and was capable of protecting British merchant ships against interception by any of Napoleon's marauders, but the risk that one of these might on some occasion succeed could never be entirely eliminated.

Hanging on another wall of Edwin's drawing-room was a sampler sewn by a young girl who was an ancestor of his. She had dated it December 8th 1808, and the sentiments it expressed – or perhaps they should be called precepts – were so similar to those conveyed by the engraving that the year 1808 could have been the date of this too.

ON INDUSTRY

Whatever you pursue, be emulous to excel. Generous ambition, and sensitivity to praise, are, especially at your age, among the marks of virtue. Think not that any affluence of fortune, or any elevation of rank, exempts you from the duties of application, or industry. Industry is the law of our being, it is the demand of nature, of reason, and of God. Remember always that the years that now pass over your head, leave permanent memorials behind them.

Maryanne Jackson December 8th. 1808.

• • •

Edwin before his bereavement had called the attention of several of his friends to the engraving over the mantelpiece and to the sampler on the side wall, and he had read out the words embroidered on the sampler to several of them. He had also commented on the similarity of their message, but after his bereavement he had never described to his friends in detail his dream of being able to enter invisibly and intangibly into the room shown in the engraving, and he hadn't mentioned to them at all the dream that followed on from the first one.

• • •

He was still able to be invisible and intangible, but the scene he was viewing was entirely different from the scene in the engraving. It was ruinous.

• • •

He found himself trapped, inextricably perhaps, beneath fallen and sharply splintered rafters. He didn't seem to have been injured, however. None of his limbs gave him any pain, and he was able to move around without too much difficulty over the rubble and wreckage that surrounded him.

After a while he discovered in the debris he trod on a prominent object which when he picked it up he recognised as a carved stone beehive from the base of the statue of Dick Whittington. But the cat Edwin found in the rubble was not the stone one that had been sculpted crouching beside Whittington's right foot; it was the formerly live cat that had looked towards him with such suspicion when he had been invisible. Now it was shrivelled and flattened, a crushed skeleton clothed in dustily matted cat's fur.

The realisation came sharply to him that he himself could become a skeleton here if he wasn't able to find a gap in the splintered rafters above him wide enough to clamber out of. He saw several gaps with white daylight visible through them, but these all looked much too narrow. He frantically searched, and at last found one which though still not quite large enough might, he thought, be widened sufficiently if he pushed with all his strength against the rafters on either side of it.

He succeeded in getting his head through it but not his shoulders; nor was he able to withdraw his head. He could see the harbour where the ship had been waiting for the elegantly dressed father who was due to start out on his adventurous voyage. No ship was there now. A group of variously armed men, two with rifles, others with sawn-off shotguns, others with iron rods or crowbars, were standing along the quay. He called desperately to them for help. They might kill him, he knew, but he would certainly die if he were left hanging from the gap beween the rafters with nothing but splintered wood to cling on to.

They heard him; and two of them, carrying crow-bars, climbed over the wreckage towards him. They didn't take long to extricate him, and after they had dragged him up into the daylight one of them asked him, 'Whose side are you on?'

'I don't know,' Edwin said, bewildered.

'Are you a scab?' the other asked.

Edwin, bewildered still, did not answer.

They seized him by his arms, forcing his head down, and they frog-marched him along the quay. A woman, whose voice he felt he was on the point of recognising, suddenly spoke to them.

'I can vouch for him,' she told them. 'He has always supported the dockers.'

The men released his arms and he was able to stand more or less upright.

He saw that the woman who had spoken was Ella, his wife.

'Oh Ella,' he said, 'how happy I am. I've been believing that you were dead.'

'No, Edwin, I am alive, though I can't feel confident that I shall survive for much longer.'

'You are too pessimistic, Ella,' one of the men holding a rifle said.

He was bulkily-bodied, ruddy-cheeked and his hair was cut so short that it stood up like stiff bristles all over his scalp. He had a West Country accent, Edwin thought. 'The Government are not the only possessors of heavy artillery,' he went on; 'we are capturing more of theirs every day. And their infantry are many of them conscripts now who are not at all keen to be here. Some of them even sympathise with us and are already surrendering with their weapons.'

The second rifle-holder, dark-haired and speaking with a middle-class accent, said to Ella, 'I hope your husband will be more optimistic than you are, but at present he is probably still too dazed by his experience of being in a house hit by a heavy shell to remember that we are engaged in a twenty-first-century revolutionary war.'

'We mustn't be too critical of her, Vernon,' the West Countryman said. 'No doubt she's tired after having to give first-aid to so many wounded comrades.'

'Yes, that's true, Jimmy,' Vernon said. 'I'm sorry, Ella.'

Edwin became aware now that she wore a blue uniform and was carrying slung over her shoulder a canvas bag with a red cross marked on it.

'When did you qualify as a nurse?' he asked her.

'I didn't,' she said. 'I never had any training in a hospital. I attended first-aid classes arranged by our local revolutionary committee. What I'm wearing isn't a nurse's uniform but only an old blue dress of mine. I don't suppose you remember it.'

'Yes I do,' he said, 'I liked it, and it seems very appropriate here.'

Gradually Edwin was beginning to remember that he was living in the twenty-first century, not the twentieth. But there were many things he remained unclear about.

'Why is the Government still using heavy artillery?' he asked Jimmy.

'It of course possesses far deadlier weapons,' Jimmy said, 'which it daren't use – such as rays that could blind thousands with a single flash, and gases and biological poisons that could kill millions.'

'The reason it doesn't use these,' Vernon said, 'is simply that, if it did, it would destroy the foundation on which the continued existence of its own upper-class supporters is based. It would deprive them of a workforce to exploit.'

'Yes, that's clear to me now,' Edwin said. 'And I would be glad to know something more about the dock strike. There is a dock strike here, isn't there?'

'Very much so,' Jimmy said, 'and not only here. It is spreading all over the country.'

'And what's very significant about it is that it's spreading in spite of the opposition of the Union leaders, who say it's illegal,' Vernon said. 'But at least there is one Dockers' Union leader who fully supports it. I mean Jimmy here.'

'Whose Law are we breaking?' Jimmy asked, and then answered his own question: 'The Law of a reactionary ruling-class which hopes that by smashing the power of the Unions it will be helped to get out of the crisis which its own rotten economic system has got it into. It aims to make the workers defenceless against a ruthless further cutting down of their already lowered standard of living.'

'But the dockers have learnt at last that the law must be broken,' Vernon said, 'as have the workers in many other industries. A central revolutionary committee has now been set up to co-ordinate the activities of all the local committees.'

'We have contacted the French central committee too,' Jimmy said, 'or rather I should say that the French central committee have contacted ours. They are in advance of us. They are already in contact with the revolutionary unions of several other countries.'

'What we still lack is a world-wide united political – as distinct from trade union – revolutionary leadership,' Vernon said.

'The Unions can create their own international revolutionary leadership,' Jimmy objected; 'they don't need professional revolutionaries from among the intelligentsia to tell them what to do.'

The development of a political argument between Vernon and Jimmy along classic lines was prevented by the beginning of what became a barrage of shells from the Government's heavy artillery.

Vernon and Jimmy with their rifles and the other men with their sawn-off shotguns or iron bars or crow-bars hurried to take cover behind the nearest undestroyed building, and Edwin and Ella followed them.

Soon the purpose of the barrage was revealed. It was to give cover for an assault by riflemen and snipers from the opposite side of the quay. These, however, finding themselves in the open, advanced with caution, each of them ready at any moment to flop into a prone position. But occasionally a sniper fired, having spotted the movement of a docker somewhere farther along the near side of the quay.

Ella crawled out with her red-crossed canvas bag in the direction towards which she thought the snipers had been firing. Edwin would have liked to dissuade her, but he knew she was doing what she ought to do.

Jimmy, after a discussion with the rest of the armed dockers who had taken shelter behind the undestroyed building, persuaded them that a successful counter-offensive was possible. They could rush the bridge and take the enemy in the rear.

He crept out from the cover of the building, reconnoitring. Then abruptly he gave the signal, and they and Edwin followed him as stooping low he ran at speed towards the enemy's bridge-head, and shooting the unalert sentry there he led them across the bridge. The enemy snipers and riflemen, surrounded from the rear, surrendered without firing a shot.

There was an argument between Jimmy and the others – which Edwin took no part in – about whether to spare their lives or not. The majority thought it might be too risky, but Jimmy insisted, saying, 'If we killed our prisoners we would be putting ourselves on the same murderous level as the Government. If we let them live, some of them may learn eventually to side with us. In the meantime we need a volunteer who will take charge of them and see that they don't try to escape.'

One of the men carrying a sawn-off shotgun offered to be responsible for them; and the argument ended.

An anxiety had all this while been growing in Edwin about Ella. He told Jimmy that he wanted to re-cross the bridge and to go and look for her.

'I will come with you,' Jimmy said.

'And I will too,' Vernon said.

On the other side of the bridge they hadn't far to walk before coming upon the dead bodies of several dockers who had been unable to find cover and had been shot by the Government snipers. But there were two wounded who had been given first-aid treatment and were sitting up.

'We'll get you to a hospital as soon as we can find one that hasn't been destroyed by the Government's gunners,' Jimmy told them, trying to sound hopeful.

'Was it Ella who bandaged you?' Edwin asked them.

'Yes, it was,' one of them answered.

Edwin hurried ahead, followed by Jimmy and Vernon. Suddenly after passing the dead bodies of two more dockers he saw the body of a woman. She was lying on her side, in a torn blue uniform. He leant over her and became sure that she was Ella and that she was dead. He wept unrestrainedly, his tears wetting her face.

'She died for the cause that means more than anything else in the world to all of us,' Jimmy said.

'She has not died in vain,' Vernon said. 'Our struggle will triumph in the end, even if it may have a long way to go yet.'

At this moment Edwin, though he fully shared Vernon's optimism, realised with extreme relief that he had only been dreaming. Ella had not been killed.

But he was strangely slow in fully awaking from the dream, almost as if he wanted to cling on to it.

Finally the dreadful reality of the twentieth-century morning broke in upon him. He remembered that Ella had died. He would be as he had been before his serial dreaming had begun. His friends would continue to invite him out to evening meals, and while he was with them he would show his gratitude by being as cheerful as he could be. Then he would return to his own lonely house.

~ THE INTANGIBLE MAN ~

MARRIED FOR fifty-five years, Adrian and Emma Shelford loved each other, and each feared death less than they feared for the one who would survive the other and might not be able to cope alone. In the fifty-sixth year of their marriage it happened that Emma died. Their two married daughters, Lucy and Sally, who grieved deeply for her, travelled down from their homes in the north and north-east of England for the burial, which their father did not attend. Nor would Emma have attended his burial if he had died first. Adrian and Emma had agreed that it would be unbearable for either of them to expose their pain publicly, even though their public would consist only of a few old political friends besides their own daughters. But Lucy and Sally, for their part, found it almost unbearable to witness a burial that in accordance with their mother's and father's wishes was without ceremony of any kind, and to take their last look at the mound of earth covering a grave over which no memorial stone would be raised. Also they were apprehensive that their father might be unable to look after himself when they had to return to their own husbands and children. But Adrian reminded them of the friends he had living locally in his London suburb, and he assured them he could cook for himself, and above all he could find consolation in continuing to give active support to the political cause which had always meant so much to him and to their mother. He spoke with such conviction that both Lucy and Sally felt a little happier about him when they had to leave him.

His belief that he would be able to cope was genuine enough, but his daughters would have been greatly alarmed if they had known how much the pain of his bereavement had upset his mental balance. An eccentric idea was beginning to occupy his thoughts more and more now. It was not new to him; it had first come to him as a young boy after he'd read H.G.Wells's *The Invisible Man*. He had tried to imagine then what would happen in a story about a man who could be seen but not felt. The sinister difference between Adrian's speculations in boyhood and in old age was that, since Emma's death, he'd been seriously trying to think up a method of making himself actually intangible. He had hardly any hope that he would succeed, but he felt that if he could it would be of inestimable value to him at a time when there were going to be exceptionally large London political demonstrations in which he would risk being injured by the police.

He did not begin to recognise this idea for the delusion it was till after Avril Linton came to live with him. She was an old friend of Emma's and shared Emma's political views. She wrote him a letter condoling with him and asking if she might come to see him. Adrian and Avril had met before but had not fully realised then how attractive they were to each other. She told him now that as a widow with a married son who worked abroad she was finding the house she lived in too large for her. She agreed when he asked her to come and share his house, which she would find comparatively small.

'I am sure Emma would have been glad for me if she could have known I would have you to live with me.'

'And I am sure Frank would have been glad that I shall be living with you,' Avril said.

Adrian wrote to Lucy and Sally telling them what had happened and inviting them to come down soon to meet Avril again.

They had known and liked her since the days in their childhood when she had come to their house to visit her old friend their mother, and they were happy that their father had got this nice woman to live with who having money of her own was obviously no gold-digger but was genuinely fond of him.

Eventually Avril's son Wilfred came over from abroad to meet Adrian for the first time, and approved of him, judging that he was comfortably off and was sharing his house with her because she was attractive to him and not because he was after her money.

When Avril had settled into Adrian's house and had at last found someone wanting to rent her own house and in her opinion unlikely to be a swindler – he was the married son of a bank manager – they felt it was high time they became politically active again.

'But why should his being the son of a bank manager make him less likely to swindle you?', Adrian asked.

'Yes, why?', she said. 'I'm afraid I've no good reason for thinking so.

The truth is that house-owning puts one in danger of becoming tainted with bourgeois prejudices.'

'That's just what the ruling-class intends to happen to working-class people who are enabled by the Government to buy the Council houses they have been living in,' he said.

'And then they become unemployed or bankrupted and are evicted for not being able to keep up their mortgage payments,' she said. 'We ought to join some of the demonstrations that are being held to prevent families from being thrown out by the bailiffs.'

'We shall have so much to do that we shall hardly know where to start,' he said.

'But we shall still have time to enjoy each other, I hope,' she said.

They both laughed. Every night they were close together in a double bed – though not the bed he had shared for years with Emma, which would have reminded him that he had everlastingly lost her and that no one else could be what she had been to him. And Avril felt that Adrian could never be to her what Frank had been. Nevertheless they had their pleasures; and these though lacking in young intensity had the advantage, often discovered by compatible elderly couples, of being long-drawn out.

Their first political activity together was reconnoitring the area where they expected to be taking part later on in big demonstrations against the Government. They were well aware that at their age it would be unwise for them to be in a police-confronting crowd for too long, and one of the objects of their reconnaissance was to familiarise Avril with the escape routes he and Emma had on occasion used. He also wanted her to see for herself something of the present abominations of everynight life in London which she, living far out in the country and not having recently travelled up to town at night, hadn't yet seen.

Adrian and Avril walked together along central London streets where almost every doorway that gave at least a little overhead protection from the weather was occupied by curled-up would-be sleepers old and young, some of them draped in newspapers or rags or sacking; and their faces, when visible, were usually filthy. But one youngish man did not look filthy and was fully awake. Avril spoke to him and asked him sympathetically whether it wasn't possible to find better free shelter anywhere.

'It is possible,' he said, in an educated voice, 'but I know what these places are like, and nothing would get me into any of them.'

He turned his face away from her, evidently determined to answer no more questions, though she would have been greatly interested to hear more about 'these places'.

They decided too that they ought to see for themselves the condition of the London Tube railways, but that they would be rash to do this late at night. Fairly early morning would be preferable, when people were beginning to go to work.

They found unswept rubbish scattered over the first platform they went down on to; and near the end of this, just inside a passageway with NO ENTRY printed in red above it, they saw the crouched figure of a man who held a blanket incompletely covering his face from which tears were dripping.

'I wish there was something we could do to help him,' Avril said.

'Yes, that's how I feel,' Adrian said.

The train they were waiting for appeared at last out of the tunnel and drew to a stop alongside the platform. The doors slid open, operated by the driver. There was no guard on the train to ensure that passengers boarded without being caught between the closing doors. There were no railway staff of any kind on the platform either.

The carriage they stepped quickly into before the doors were shut seemed very crowded. Adrian and Avril did not try to find seats but stayed together by the doors. At the next station they got out, voluntarily, though they might have been pushed out anyway by the huddled group of other passengers pressing behind them. Most of these overtook them in the general movement towards the escalator, near the base of which were a few cigarette ends and other discarded rubbish of the sort that had probably contributed to the disastrous fire at another Tube station not so many months ago. Adrian and Avril weren't sorry when the escalator brought them up to ground level at the top and they could make for the exit to the street; but just before they reached the exit a tall black man spoke to them.

'Could you spare me the money for a cup of coffee?' he asked.

He spoke in a pathetically humble voice. Avril surprised herself as well as Adrian by producing her purse from her bag and giving him money. The tall man after receiving this thanked her effusively and bowing low to her he embarrassingly took hold of her hand and kissed it. Then they left him, and were relieved to get out into the street.

'He made me feel so awkward and so inferior,' Avril said. 'Even the misery I thought I could never recover from when Frank died seems minor in comparison with what he must have to go through every day.'

'I don't expect he will starve, even if he spends the money on drugs,' Adrian said, 'and most of our woes in this country so far are as nothing compared with the sufferings of the hundreds of thousands who face famine in the third world.'

'We must try to help them by making the best political use we can of our good luck,' she said.

'Yes,' he said, 'charity will never solve their problem, any more than what you gave the black man will solve his.'

'No, though I'm not sorry I gave it, and I'm glad there are charities that bring food to at least some of the third world people who are starving.'

'But we know that until the governments of the rich world are forced to act or are overthrown to make way for governments that will, the problem of famine won't begin to be solved.'

'That's true, of course,' she said.

'As for my good luck, I don't think I've ever told you that after Emma died, and before you came to live with me, I was suffering from an insane delusion for a while,' he said.

'I knew you'd been under great stress, but you didn't give the impression of being at all near to insanity.'

'That was because meeting you had already begun to cure me. My delusion was that I might be able to make myself intangible, a very useful accomplishment if I were attacked by policemen during a demonstration.'

'How did you try to become intangible?' she asked

'By a kind of auto-hypnosis. I used to sit in an armchair and say to myself over and over again, "I am gradually becoming intangible", and after a few minutes I would tell myself, "I have become intangible".

Then I would abandon the exercise, hoping that with a little more practice I would be able whenever necessary to make myself invulnerable instantly to any attack.'

'Did you think of the effect that this, if you were successful, would be likely to have on a policeman who batoned or tried to arrest you?'

'I didn't,' he said. 'I suppose if I had thought about it I would have expected the policeman to believe he'd been hallucinating and to decide that he would do his prospects in the force no good by mentioning the event to any of his colleagues.'

'Or he might have decided that he hadn't been hallucinating and that you were a character with dangerous powers who must be destroyed at any cost. And one day you could have been shot through the heart by a police sniper before you'd had time to make youself invulnerable.'

'If I'd thought of that I would have given myself the power not merely to make my tangible body intangible but also to revive it if it was killed.'

'In other words you would have made your spiritual self capable of surviving your body and of raising it from the dead.'

'That's right,' he said.

'Let's hope neither of us gets truncheoned or destroyed in reality,' she said.

'We will be rather less at risk now that I have given up all hope of making myself invulnerable,' he said. 'I have quite recovered from my "insane delusion". Thanks to you.'

They were walking along the pavement to get a bus back to their suburban home. They laughed. They felt a little better now than they had before leaving the Tube.

• • •

THE FIRST DEMONSTRATION they went to together was the first that had been organised by UCAR, the United Campaign Against Racism. It was in Hyde Park on a warm late September Sunday afternoon. Their taxi-driver set them down at the Grosvenor Gate (the bus journey here would have been roundabout and lengthy for them), and they walked from the Gate towards the central grassy site where the meeting was already in progress. The crowd round the well-known left-wing Labour speaker, John Bedford, who stood above it on a portable platform, was not as large as they'd hoped it would be but it was larger than it might have been, considering such counter-attractions as boating on the Serpentine or sitting in deck-chairs beside the sunny water there. Very few policemen were visible. Presumably they were not expecting trouble, though in any case they could no doubt get reinforcements if needed from the police station out of sight downhill not far from the Serpentine. Adrian and Avril were glad to see among the listeners to Bedford a number of blacks – a sign that UCAR was not just a middle-class movement trying to defend ethnic minorities without their active support. Bedford was forcefully stating his view that the recently formed New Nationalist Party of Britain was a neo-Nazi party under another name and that it ought to be banned. Adrian and Avril hoped that he would be followed by a black speaker who would support him. Then as they stood listening at the back of the crowd they became conscious that Keith Clandon, the Conservative Member of Parliament for the suburb where they lived, was standing quite close to them. Adrian spoke to him.

'Mr Clandon, I think.'

'Yes, I am.' Clandon spoke with a slight chilliness which suggested that Adrian's 'I think' had put him on his guard.

'We are constituents of yours,' Avril said, 'though we haven't been in touch with you before.'

'We would like to take the opportunity now of asking what you think about the New Nationalist Party of Britain,' Adrian said.

Clandon relaxed. 'I can answer you quite simply,' he said. 'I detest them.'

'Would you agree that your Government ought to ban them?' Avril asked.

'Definitely not,' Clandon said. 'If they were illegalised they would merely be driven underground where surveillance of their activities would become less easy. And in any case to deny them the right of free speech would be to behave more like Stalinists,' – he paused to give Adrian and Avril a keenly suspicious look – 'than like the elected Government of a democratic country.'

'Do you accept John Bedford's view that the New Nationalist Party are really neo-Nazis under another name?' Avril asked.

'No, I do not,' Clandon said. 'I accept their own statement that they are an entirely independent British Party. But of course I would approve of severe punishment for any of their members who broke the law by coming out publicly with virulent racist propaganda.'

Adrian asked, 'Isn't it true that an increase of racial conflict could help to deflect from the Government some of the popular anger caused by its policies on local taxation and health and housing and unemployment and education?'

'I am not in the habit of wasting my time talking to people who make defamatory insinuations of this kind about the Government,' Clandon said huffily, and he turned his back on them and walked away.

A young man standing nearby said to them, 'I couldn't help overhearing your argument with Clandon. What a twit the man is.'

'He is certainly no supporter of UCAR,' Avril said.

'Nor am I, altogether,' the young man said, 'though I sympathise with their intentions. They are too broad an organisation to be able to act strongly enough against the New Nationalists. They even have a member of the Tory Party as one of their members.'

'We support UCAR,' Adrian said, 'and we believe that the more converts it can make from diverse groups the more effective it will be.'

'Only the industrial working class in alliance with a genuine Marxist party can finally defeat the neo-Nazi racists,' the young man said.

'Finally, yes,' Avril said, 'but in the meantime Marxists should support not oppose this non-Marxist non-party campaign.'

The argument did not continue. There was a disturbance close to the platform from which John Bedford was speaking. A small fight seemed to have broken out, and the young man left them and pushed his way through the crowd towards it. Quite soon it stopped, but he did not return to them. Two other people did come out of the crowd to speak to them, however – Vee and Patrick Elmfield.

'How good to see you here,' Vee said admiringly to Adrian. She turned to Patrick with the comment, 'He doesn't look a day older than sixty, does he?'

'No, he doesn't,' Patrick agreed.

'I've been told this so often that I've almost begun to believe it,' Adrian said. 'But let me introduce Avril to you. She is an old friend of Emma's, and we are living together now.' Then he said to Avril, 'These are Vee and Patrick. I've talked to you about them, you'll remember.'

Vee and Patrick shook hands with Avril. Patrick asked her, 'What do you think of this UCAR meeting? '

'I think it is a good first effort to reach the general public.'

'Vee and I are uneasy about it,' Patrick said.

'We think Bedford should have stated at the start of his speech that UCAR is a non-violent as well as a non-party campaign,' Vee said.

'Avril and I didn't arrive in time to hear the beginning of the speech,' Adrian said, 'but wasn't it obvious that supporters of UCAR were unlikely to be tempted to commit acts of violence today in the Park? I would agree of course that before a UCAR street demonstration which could be infiltrated by police provocateurs it would be essential to warn the demonstrators not to let themselves be provoked.'

'But there has been violence by UCAR supporters at this present meeting,' Vee said. 'They manhandled a skinhead wearing a neo-Nazi tee-shirt who tried to push Bedford's platform over.'

'Would you have been in favour of letting him push it over?' Avril asked.

'No, I would have been in favour of holding the platform so that he couldn't push it over,' Vee said.

'I'm afraid you would have risked getting some hefty heavy-booted kicks if you had done that,' Adrian said.

'I would have been aware I might have to take physical blows but I hope I would have had the physical courage to take them without trying to hit back.'

'And what would you do if you were charged by mounted police, as any of us well may be in future demonstrations?', Avril asked.

'I have to admit I don't believe I'm of the stuff true martyrs are made of,' Vee said, 'and I should probably run away if I could.'

'I think it might sometimes be tactically advisable to run away,' Adrian said, 'and to fight another day – or the same day later on.'

'It might be justifiable to run from a police charge if we could,' Patrick said, 'but not to fight another day'. 'We believe in passive resistance.'

'Suppose a racist New Nationalist Party government were elected in this country,' Adrian said, 'and were secretly employing death squads to eliminate opposition, would you refuse to support a resistance movement which actively counterattacked such a government?'

'Perhaps such a government is less likely to be elected here,' Avril said, 'than a more traditional one which would introduce into this country in a still more vicious form the methods that have been used to maintain Britain's control over Northern Ireland.'

'We would refuse to take part in violence of any kind in any circumstances,' Patrick said. 'We would support the peace-makers.'

'They will always fail,' Adrian said, 'so long as the world is dominated by people who live by exploiting others.'

'But violence will never be ended by violence,' Vee said. 'It will end only when the great majority of the world's people have learnt the lesson that it must end.'

• • •

BEFORE ADRIAN OR AVRIL could begin to pursue the argument in any greater political or philosophical depth Patrick said, 'I'm afraid we shall have to leave you. A friend of ours has arranged to meet us at the Victoria Gate in about ten minutes from now.'

'We must see you both again quite soon,' Vee said.

Adrian told Avril with a laugh after the other two had left them, 'I'm glad they were the first to give up the argument. I've been feeling I couldn't go on standing here much longer.'

'Well, let's get a bus home,' Avril suggested.

'It's a pity we shan't hear the rest of the the speeches,' Adrian said, 'and the meeting will no doubt be ignored by the media, because it was neither remarkably large nor was it small enough to be described as a total failure. Also the one slightly violent incident in it was too insignificant to be called a riot.'

'I don't think they are likely to ignore our future demonstrations,' Avril said.

• • •

THE NEXT UCAR demonstration they joined was against a New Nationalist Party march to Trafalgar Square. The police, who had given permission for this, were conspicuously present with the obvious intention of clearing a way for the marchers through the many thousands of UCAR supporters who aimed at nonviolently obstructing the NNP from holding a meeting in the Square. And less conspicuously the riot-police carrying transparent plastic shields, and the mounted police with leather-holstered long batons attached to their horses' saddles, were waiting in certain side streets.

It seemed to Adrian and Avril that considerable police violence was probable, and they realised that they must think out quickly which would be their best escape route. They decided to walk away from the Square immediately and to try to get past and beyond the advancing racist march.

'According to Emma,' Adrian told Avril, 'the worst thing you can do if you want to avoid being beaten up by the police in situations like this is to stand close to a wall. That simply makes any escape quite impossible for you.'

No one prevented them from walking back along the pavement towards and then past the few hundred advancing NNP marchers, who did not shout insults at them and were mostly youngish males ordinary enough in appearance except for the look of fixed aggressiveness their faces had; but some way beyond the rear of the march three rows of policemen were drawn up across the road. A police sergeant brusquely beckoned to Adrian and Avril to come forward along the pavement and to pass round one of the flanks of these rows, which they did, and on the far side they found themselves among a very large crowd whose banners and placards showed support for UCAR.

New contingents were steadily continuing to arrive. It became clear to Adrian and Avril that the police plan was to prevent the UCAR supporters here from reinforcing those who were already massed on and in front of the Square ahead. The increasing crowd were already becoming more and more impatient, when suddenly they and Adrian and Avril heard from the direction of the Square the unmistakable sound made by the riot-police beating their shields with their batons and yelling an incoherent wordless war-cry before charging the unarmed UCAR supporters there. From the Square the sound of screams and of outraged shouting rose high above the hoof-clatter of the horses ridden by the mounted police who had joined in the charge. The crowd pressed forward against the first of the three rows of policemen, yet somehow Adrian and Avril were able to resist being swept forward; they even managed to move in an opposite direction and to get out on to a crowdless section of the road. But all at once just behind them there was a crash of glass on the road surface and a simultaneous burst of flame which was close enough for them to feel something of its intense heat without actually being burnt by it. A milk-bottle petrol bomb it must have been, they thought, thrown by an enemy of UCAR intending it to explode in the middle of the crowd who were pressing against the three rows of police, but it had fallen short, and the thrower had quickly disappeared by a pre-planned route. Adrian and Avril hurried on away from what had happened, and they thought themselves extremely lucky when they found an unengaged taxi whose driver was willing to take them home.

After they had been sitting in it for a while and had recovered their breath a little, Adrian said, 'It's interesting to realise that if that bomb had dropped a yard or two nearer I could have become a genuinely intangible man.'

'Yes,' Avril said, 'and I could have become an equally intangible woman.'

They were glad to reach home again, and to eat a small supper before they went early to bed together. Neither of them could get to sleep, and before long Adrian began to complain of a pain in his stomach.

'It's your nerves after our experience at the demo,' she said.

But his pain became steadily more acute, and at last Avril phoned for a doctor, who arrived fairly promptly. He was the one who happened to be on duty, not their usual doctor in the partnership.

He examined Adrian with as much care as their own doctor would have done, and then he asked to use their telephone to make an urgent call for an ambulance.

•

If the traffic around London had been less congested the ambulance might have reached the house more quickly and have taken Adrian to the hospital in time to save his life, but he died from heart failure soon after arriving there. Avril, who had come with him in the ambulance, was able to stay the night in the hospital under sedation before returning alone to their home the next day.

•

She could not bear to attend the funeral service that Adrian's daughters arranged, though she raised no objection to it, and she parted on good terms with them.

• • •

SHE AND ADRIAN had always been just as aware as she and Frank and as Emma and Adrian had been of how difficult it would be for the survivor to go on living without the other. And Avril was the only one of the four to become a survivor twice over.

But she had learnt from Adrian's experience to be on guard against delusion, which in her case might have taken the form of believing the pain of her new bereavement to be too great for her to hope she could ever lessen it.

•

She succeeded in avoiding this delusion by making up her mind to continue to help in whatever way she was still capable of the cause that he and Frank and Emma had never deserted.

~ A BETTER JOB ~

ON AN UNSWEPT railway station platform conspicuously littered with dropped cigarette ends and muddy scraps of trodden newspaper, Maurice Prichard had waited at least twenty minutes before deciding to go and look for someone who might know why the train he wanted to catch was so late.

There were no station staff – the private company which had bought this railway had dispensed with them in the interests of economy – so he went out to a nearby pub, where one of the drinkers suggested that the delay might be due to a fault in the signalling system.

'It has happened before,' another drinker said.

The landlord of the pub added grimly, 'By good luck there's been no serious accident on this line yet.'

Maurice asked the drinkers in general: 'How long would you think they'll take to do the repairs?'

'Two hours or more,' a cheery-voiced man estimated. 'What about you having a few drinks with us while you wait?'

'That's a very pleasant proposal,' Maurice answered, 'but I feel I would like to explore the country round here for a bit; it looks interesting.'

Nobody spoke as he turned and, giving them all an amiable good-bye wave of the hand, walked out of the pub.

• • •

HE FOUND HIMSELF in a valley with a pebbly stream meandering along it. At right-angles to this was a high grass-covered hill. He chose to climb the hill, which became steeper as he climbed. Wild flowers were growing in the grass and he paused to try to identify them; but he could not immediately remember any of their names. Then, as he continued his climb, the hill became yet steeper, and he was glad to find soft grass to sit on when he at last reached the summit.

• • •

HE WAS SURPRISED by the view he got from it. He had difficulty in deciding whether what he saw distantly below him could be more truly described as houses among trees or as trees among houses. And what were the large horizontal buildings in a semi-circle beyond the trees and houses? His guess was that they might be smokeless modern factories. But he was in little doubt that the broad band of green and brown land which seemed to make a complete circle surrounding everything, including even the hill he sat on, must be agricultural land.

After resting for a while he stood up from the grass and began to walk down towards the houses and the trees.

The descent was steep, though less so than the ascent, and he was on level ground when he reached a small bridge spanning a water-filled ditch. Not far beyond the bridge stood a ten-foot high stone; it was obelisk-shaped, reddish in colour and smoothly polished, and across the wide base of it were incised the words, WELCOME TO THE THIRD GARDEN CITY.

•

At the moment when he stepped off the bridge he was approached by a grey-haired middle-aged black man in baggy navy-blue trousers and a brown tweed jacket, who said to him, 'Can I help you?'

His tone as he said this made Maurice ask, 'Am I trespassing?'

'No. But you are rather smartly dressed. Are you a Government-appointed Inspector by any chance?'

'Certainly not,' Maurice said. Then he remembered that he had put on his best suit this morning in order to avoid giving an unfavourable first impression to the committee who would be interviewing him for the post of deputy-head at a prestigious school.

He tried to tell the black man briefly why he was wearing a smart suit, and also to explain that he'd decided to go on this country walk only because the train he needed to catch was likely to be at least two hours late.

'Did you intentionally go in the direction of this Garden City?' the black man asked.

'No, I didn't.'

'Had you ever heard of us?'

'I am ashamed to say I hadn't.'

'We are in many ways different from Letchworth and Welwyn. Have you heard of those?'

'Yes, and I've talked to my Sixth Form about them. I much admire Ebenezer Howard for his conception of towns that would be both residential and industrial, and would be surrounded by agricultural land.'

'The world today has changed somewhat since he had that admirable idea,' the black man said. 'You've no doubt noticed the ditch beneath this bridge that you have just crossed?'

'Of course.'

'But you may not have guessed its purpose, perhaps.'

'No, I haven't.'

'We've had it dug to encircle the City completely so that traffic from outside is able to enter only by one or other of our four bridges over it. We can exclude air-polluting petrol and diesel vehicles of all kinds, while readily accepting electrically-powered cars and vans and farmers' horse-drawn carts.'

'I think that's very good,' Maurice said, 'though I suppose you must have met with some opposition to it?'

'We have, indeed. We are disapproved of by various important business firms – and by the Government.'

'Why by the Government?' Maurice asked.

'For one thing, because Governments in general tend to support big firms, as you may be aware.'

'I am.'

'Also the present Government particularly dislikes us because we are making a success of a planned economy, and they are fanatical believers in giving full rein to market forces. But as we are a perfectly legal organisation and they are not fascist dictators – at least not yet – they adopt surreptitious tactics against us. A few acts of sabotage here have been perpetrated mainly, we suspect, by their MI5 undercover agents.'

'What sort of sabotage?'

'Well, – to mention a comparatively minor sort – substituting tins of food which are long past their sell-by date for the fresh tins we have on the shelves of one of our most popular shops. We have caught and expelled several such agents.'

'Is that all you can do to them?'

'We could hardly establish our own prisons to put them in. That would give the Government an excellent pretext for arresting every member of our Leading Committee.'

'Leading Committee?'

'Yes. The inhabitants of this Garden City are a self governing co-operative and they have elected a Committee to organise necessary services for the community as a whole. I have been entrusted by the Committee recently with the job of Marshal, as it's called, and my main duty is to keep an eye open for ill-intentioned intruders here. I can be sacked at any time if I fail to do my job efficiently.'

'I hope that my asking so many questions hasn't made you wonder whether I might be one of those intruders,' Maurice said more than half seriously.

'A favourite principle of mine,' the Marshal answered,' is to trust no one absolutely, but if useful things are to get done the doers should be trusted for as long as they continue doing them competently.'

'I would very much like to do something for you before I have to catch my train,' Maurice said.

'Then let me show you all I can of our Garden City, on condition that, when you get back to the ghastly "free world" you work in, you will tell the truth about us.'

'I promise to do that.'

'Very well, I'll take you first to look at some of our houses.'

Maurice was led by the Marshal towards that part of the City which, when he had viewed it from the summit of the hill, he had found difficulty in deciding whether it consisted of houses among trees or of trees among houses.

He felt a sudden intense happiness. The memory came to him from many years before of going on a Sunday ramble in the country not many miles from London with a small group of young men and women. They passed a medium-sized red-brick Edwardian house partly screened by a few trees, silver birches perhaps, with slim trunks which did not prevent him from clearly seeing the verandah of the house. And the French windows leading out to the verandah from the room behind were wide open, revealing a handsome casually-dressed youngish man who was pouring white wine from a long-necked bottle into a tall glass. And there was laughter in the room.

The happiness that was aroused in Maurice by the memory of this, and of the girls and men who had been with him then, remained strong in him as he neared the red-brick houses which the Marshal was taking him to see.

The gardens of these houses were as large as the groups of trees among which they were placed. The trees were various – mainly beech, oak and ash – and the houses, though none were semi-detached, were of different sizes, some of them quite a lot larger than most of the others.

'Does this mean that there are inhabitants of this City who are better off financially than the majority?' Maurice asked.

The Marshal turned on him with scorn. 'No,' he said, 'it means that some of our people need larger houses – if they have larger families, for instance.'

'I should have guessed that,' Maurice said, momentarily abashed. Then suddenly he asked, 'How did you learn to speak like an educated man?'

'Not in your world, except negatively,' the Marshal said, seemingly without displeasure at being given an excuse to talk about himself for a change. 'Your world was the world I was born into, and went to a rotten school in. I was lucky to find one or two badly paid temporary jobs and lastly I became a dustman for the Council. They provided me and my wife and three children with a top floor flat on a Council estate. But early one night when I happened to go out for a stroll someone pushed an ignited petrol-soaked rag through our letter slit into our hall and my wife and three children were burnt to death before the firemen could arrive.'

•

'It was when I was feeling suicidal soon after this that one of the Councillors, a woman who wished me well, advised me to go and live and work for a while in the Third Garden City and then to return to the district where I was born and to join the fight against Racism there. I may yet do this.'

Maurice was silent.

'You were asking me where I got my education,' the Marshal said. 'The answer is that I got it at our own excellent university here. I have a degree in philosophy and politics.'

'Now let me take you to our biggest shop,' the Marshal said. 'We call it The Stores, and you will find that it is not at all an ordinary shop. It contains a first-rate restaurant and a sauna and a Jacuzzi, besides having a spacious lounge and a library.'

On their way to The Stores, Maurice remembered the Marshal's remark that the larger houses were for people with larger families. He now reminded the Marshal of this and asked him, 'What sort of education is provided for children in this City?'

'There is nothing avant-garde about it,' the Marshal said. 'Besides some elementary world history and geography they are taught the three r's. But they are not reproved for being slow to master English spelling, which is more ridiculously irrational than the spelling in any other language.'

'Are you inspected by Government Inspectors?'

'We are,' the Marshal said. 'Only because we ask to be. It isn't compulsory, as our schools are not state schools. And, to the chagrin of the Government, the Inspectors have shown honourable independence and have produced very favourable reports on all our schools.'

'And what about public health?'

'We have our own medical school, and of course our own hospital.'

'What is the Government's attitude to this?'

'Unhelpful, to say the least. However, there is nothing to prevent any of our medical students from going out into your corrupt world if they wish, and continuing their studies there.'

'Who pays for that?'

'We do. But would you like to try our restaurant, where we could carry on our conversation more comfortably?'

'Yes, thanks very much, I would.'

It was a large bright room, though well shaded from direct sunlight. Maurice praised this as they came into it, and the Marshal told him that in dull weather it was kept just as bright by indirect electric lighting.

'Incidentally, what would you say to our having a pre-prandial in the sitting-room before we eat?' the Marshal asked.

'I would certainly like one,' Maurice said.

'Is there any you would particularly like?'

'Just a dry sherry, please.'

The Marshal made a sign to a middle-aged white man wearing a cream-coloured jacket, who then approached them with a friendly smile.

'Wilf,' the Marshal said, 'let me introduce – by the way, what is your name?' He turned to Maurice, who answered, 'Maurice Prichard,' and the Marshal went on, 'let me introduce Wilf Marston to you.' Wilf shook hands with Maurice.

'Wilf, would you bring Maurice a dry sherry,' the Marshal asked, 'and I would like an iced Campari and tonic, please.'

After Wilf had gone to fetch these pre-prandials, the Marshal said to Maurice, 'I think you will be interested to know that he was a director on the board of a very successful firm of advertisers in your world but he decided to come and live and work in our Garden City.'

'Is he married?'

'Yes, and his wife, Ellen, is as enthusiastic as he is about the life that can be lived here. Their two sons, however, have emigrated to America, although remaining on good terms with them.'

At this point Wilf Marston arrived, balancing expertly on the fingers of one hand a silvery salver from which with his other hand he passed a dry sherry to Maurice and then an iced Campari and tonic to the Marshal.

'That's wonderful,' Maurice couldn't resist exclaiming.

'It is,' Wilf grinningly agreed, 'but it took time to learn.'

A younger waiter, rather dark-complexioned and possibly an Italian, Maurice thought, who was wearing the same kind of cream-coloured jacket as Wilf wore, came to them soon, and with a slight bow to each of them presented each with the menu for lunch.'

'How are you liking this job, Gary?' the Marshal asked him.

'After months of being unemployed or doing short sham training jobs under employers well paid for helping the Government to claim to be reducing unemployment,' Gary said, 'I am very glad of it.'

The Marshal, turning to Maurice, said, 'We have no unemployment here, because there are always socially useful jobs which need doing.'

'I can think of two jobs that I wouldn't blame anyone for being unwilling to do,' Maurice said.

'And what are those?' Marshal asked.

'The job of a slaughterhouse worker or of a policeman,' Maurice answered.

'Take a good look at the menu,' the Marshal said, ignoring Maurice's linking of a policeman's job with a slaughterman's, 'and make sure you don't choose anything derived from a killed or living animal.'

'Plenty of innocent starters here,' Maurice commented. 'Vegetable soup, Grapefruit, Mango, something stuffed with Olives. I hardly know which to decide on – all of them seem extremely tempting. (It was typical of Maurice to give audible expression to his indecisions.) Gary helped him out by saying, 'I would particularly recommend the soup; it is the chef's special today.'

'All right, I'll start with the soup then,' Maurice said.

'It occurs to me,' the Marshal said to Gary, 'that it might not be quite the correct practice for waiters to suggest what choices their customers should make.'

Gary blushed.

'I may be wrong,' the Marshal said, sorry perhaps at having embarrassed him. 'And I'll have the grapefruit, please.'

After Gary had gone away to fetch the starters, the Marshal said, 'What would you like from the rest of the menu?'

Maurice read, not aloud: Pasta twists with asparagus and pea sauce; Creamy basil sauce with 'butterfly' pasta and green beans; Nut cutlets; Cheese tortelloni in mushroom sauce – but when he came to this he couldn't refrain from saying aloud, 'Doesn't cheese come from milk, doesn't milk come from cows, and aren't cows, not to mention their calves, slaughtered?'

'Our milk isn't derived from animals of any kind, or from humans for that matter,' the Marshal answered. 'I can see I have a lot to explain to you yet – but here comes Gary with the starters.'

When they had both finished their starters, the Marshal told Gary he would like to see the wine list, and having received and glanced down it he asked Maurice, 'What would you say to a half bottle of Mouton-Rothschild between us?'

'That is a very distinguished wine,' Maurice said (thinking, 'and very expensive'). He added aloud, 'I would love it.'

The Marshal, easily guessing his thought, said, 'Merchants inhabiting the world outside our City are aware that our industrial products are mostly much more reliable than theirs, and they are only too pleased to sell us their best products cheaply in exchange for what they want from us.'

Maurice, looking again at the main course section of the menu, told Gary he would like Pasta twists with asparagus and pea sauce. The Marshal significantly chose Cheese tortelloni.

Before Gary returned with what they'd ordered, the Marshal had time to tell Maurice that scientists had long known how to produce milk directly from grass without the intervention of cows at all, and that their recipe was used here in this Garden City.

'Then why isn't it in general use elsewhere?' Maurice asked.

'Really, Maurice,' the Marshal said, 'you make me feel almost like Sherlock Holmes talking to an obtuse Dr Watson. Obviously many farmers, rich as well as poor, would be ruined by it, and so would big combines like United Dairies.'

'Yes, I do admit my question was rather a slow-witted one,' Maurice said, 'but everything here is so new to me.'

'Well,' the Marshal said amiably, 'I think you may know of the discovery that soya flour can be made to taste like meat of any kind, and can be shaped like almost any joint, and is just as nutritious, and never tough or likely to cause mad cow disease. So you will readily understand why the butchers, small and big, in your world are utterly against it.'

•

They went to the sitting-room after their meal, and the Marshal ordered two tawny ports from a waiter who was neither Gary nor Wilf Marston but, as the Marshal told Maurice later, a retired Rear-Admiral who bore a grudge against the Admiralty. When he came back into the sitting-room with the two tawny ports, his face looked morose, and the Marshal did not introduce Maurice to him. After he had gone the Marshal explained to Maurice, 'He doesn't approve of strangers being brought into the City.'

•

They finished drinking their port. 'Did you like it?' the Marshal asked.

'Very much. Tawny port is the only one I do like, and this one was especially likeable.' And no doubt especially expensive too, Maurice thought.

'Good,' the Marshal said. 'Now I'll take you to see the houses again and point out certain interesting things about them that I didn't when I took you to them before.'

The Marshal brought him to a stop in front of a medium-sized red-brick house and said, 'Have a look at the roof of this one. Does anything strike you as unusual about it?'

'It has three large solar panels on it.'

'Quite right. Anything else?'

'From one side of the roof a white rod goes high up into the air and at the top of this there is a small swivelling barrel-shaped object with revolving propeller-like blades attached to it.'

'Not too bad a description,' the Marshal said, 'but I suspect that though you may know what its function is you've forgotten its name.'

'I'm afraid that's true,' Maurice admitted.

'It is called a "wind generator",' the Marshal said, 'a somewhat ambiguous-sounding name – and every house here has one or more, according to the size of the house. Almost all the heat and power these houses require can be supplied by their wind generators and solar panels.'

'Why do you say almost?', Maurice asked.

'Because on rare occasions the houses have to borrow from the really big generators that supply the factories.'

'Where are these really big ones?'

'They stand at wide intervals along the circumference of the City's agricultural territory.'

'Are there no complaints from your farmers against the noise they make?'

'None. If the towers were massed together it would be another matter, but the noise produced by one of these tall generators on its own is almost negligible and is silenced altogether at night when the factories aren't working. What's more, the high voltage cables that connect them are buried underground and don't deface the countryside.'

'How does the Government react to all this?'

'They hate it, of course,' the Marshal said, 'but they find themselves in an ironic quandary: having encouraged the privatisation of the rest of the electric power-producing industry, and helped to split up the ownership of it among a number of different companies, how could they possibly justify re-introducing nationalisation and Government control in the case of our particular private industry? They have been bitten by their own ugly Rottweiler.'

'Good,' Maurice said. 'And there is one other thing I have just thought of asking about. Water. Where does this City get its water from?'

'Owing to a lucky geological arrangement of the rocks beneath us we have as much pure water available to us from underground as we shall ever want.'

'Very like London,' Maurice said.

'Yes,' the Marshal said, 'though on a rather smaller scale.'

'Oh, and there's something else that has suddenly struck me. I see no signs of religion here – no churches or mosques or synagogues.'

'I can quite simply account for this. We have a number of ex-Christians here – I am one of them – and ex-Muslims and ex-Jews and ex-Hindus who all of us have rejected the religions we were brought up to believe in, and we live and work very amicably together. You would find no religious or racial hatred in our factories, or outside them either.'

'How admirable,' Maurice said.

'Yes,' the Marshal said. 'But it occurs to me that there is one important thing you still haven't asked me about: physical exercise. Let me tell you that we have an extensive park where nearly any kind of sport can be indulged in, from tennis and football to bowls and athletics.'

•

'Now we will go to see the inside of one of the houses here. As a foretaste of the remarkable variety we get among our inhabitants I will introduce you to a couple who like to play at living in the early years of the twentieth century. The husband, Aubrey Sheldon, founded our Historical Society, and his wife Iris is an expert on Art Nouveau. See if you can spot their house from outside. Ah, here we are already at their front door.'

Maurice saw that the upper half of this door contained a stained-glass window which pictured the Blessèd Damozel leaning out from the gold bar of Heaven as in Dante Gabriel Rossetti's painting.

The Marshal pressed the bell-push beside the door and immediately a melody from a violin concerto by Saint-Saens was mechanically played somewhere inside the house.

Then the door was opened by a plump and smiling ruddy-faced white man who looked a little more than middle-aged and was wearing a bright green jacket and a flower-patterned waistcoat and beige-coloured trousers with small diamond-shaped black checks on them. All this Maurice had time to notice before the Marshal spoke:

'Please forgive us, Aubrey, for arriving so suddenly without forewarning you.'

'What utter garbage, Finn' (so this was the Marshal's real name), 'you are perfectly well aware that you and any friend or friends you may bring with you are welcome at any time, or nearly any time.'

'And is this one of the auspicious times?' Finn asked.

'Stop twaddling and come in at once,' Aubrey said.

•

Finn introduced Maurice to Aubrey, who then led them both into a room in which the furniture was antique and not at all Art Nouveau. Perhaps this was the room that he and his wife used when they were being serious and not playing at living in the early years of the twentieth century.

Aubrey called out loudly: 'Iris! We have Finn here with a new friend – Maurice Prichard.'

'Send him upstairs,' Iris called back. 'I'm not ready to come down yet.'

Maurice, a little nervously, went up the stairs and, reaching the top, he turned and was faced by smiling Iris who was wearing a dressing-gown and standing just inside the doorway of her room.

'Don't hesitate to come in,' she said. She stood aside for him and he cautiously went into the room. He saw a double bed covered with an eiderdown that had a curving purplish-blue pattern on it. He saw a marble-surfaced washhand-stand on which a similarly patterned porcelain basin and ewer stood. Suddenly she seized the lapels of his jacket and exclaimed, 'What is this ridiculous suit you are wearing?'

In spite of a lack of co-operation from him which came near to being a positive resistance, she tightly gripped his right lapel and pushing it backwards she lifted the whole shoulder of his jacket off his own shoulder and let it fall behind him, exposing his white-shirted right arm. After this she easily stripped off his entire jacket, which she was careful however to save from falling on to the floor, cleanly carpeted though this seemed to be.

As she neatly folded the jacket and placed it on a chair, she said, 'Well, Maurice, you look better now, don't you think?'

Maurice was silent.

'Perhaps you would like me to take a few more clothes off you?' Iris asked.

'Please, no,' Maurice said in alarm.

'You are a bit of a Puritan, aren't you, Maurice?'

'Yes, politically speaking, I am.'

'Fair enough. But would I be wrong in taking this to mean that, unpolitically speaking you would admit to a liking for physical love?'

Again Maurice was silent.

'You are shy perhaps?' she said. 'Never mind; let me set you an example.'

She flung her dressing-gown off on to the bed and stood up naked in front of him. Her well-preserved, shapely body keenly excited him. But he was able to restrain himself from giving any obvious physical sign of how he felt, and he asked, 'What would your husband think about this?'

'He believes in Free Love just as fervently as I do, and neither of us is ever jealous of the other. "Thou shalt not be jealous" is the first commandment for all true Free Lovers, and we think that any of us who breaks it deserves to be cast out into loveless darkness for ever.'

But Maurice was still not finally persuaded to surrender to her: 'Suppose you became pregnant,' he said.

'I am past that,' Iris said, 'and Aubrey has been infertile, though far from impotent, ever since his prostate operation. And in any case what's wrong with Free Love that produces children? They are well loved and looked after in our Third Garden City.'

He gave up resisting as she busied herself in removing the remainder of his clothes. 'You have a beautiful body,' she said, when she had made him quite naked in front of her.

She put her arms gently around him and he and she fell unclothed together on to the purplish-blue eiderdown.

She was an expert lover, though in spite of the extreme pleasure she gave him he felt a guilt which, nevertheless, strangely seemed after a while to make his pleasure even more exquisite.

At last he said, 'I wish this could go on for ever, but I'm afraid that Finn may be getting a little impatient. I know he has at least one other of the City's inhabitants he wants me to meet.'

'Very well,' Iris said, not in the least piqued, 'let us get dressed and go downstairs.'

•

They found Finn and Aubrey sitting on a comfortable-looking non-Art Nouveau sofa and talking. 'Maurice feels,' Iris said to Finn, 'that you will be impatient to take him along to visit one other of the City's inhabitants you are keen for him to meet.'

Finn gave Maurice a quick wink before saying to Iris, 'Well, my dear, happy though I am to have introduced you to Maurice, and much though I have enjoyed talking with Aubrey, perhaps the time has come for us to move on and to visit Fred Dawlish.'

'So that's who you are going to meet,' Iris remarked with interest. When Maurice and Finn said goodbye to Iris and to Aubrey at the stained-glass front door of their house, Finn added, 'See you again soon.'

•

'There are several things I need to tell you about Frederick Dawlish before you meet him,' Finn said to Maurice as they were on their way towards his house. 'Perhaps not the least important thing is that his house, by Third Garden City standards, is quite unextraordinary, though he himself is an extraordinary man, with very many admirers here. But he is modest and deplores ostentation. I wonder whether you have heard of him?'

'I don't think I ever have,' Maurice admitted.

'Milton somewhere in *Paradise Lost*, makes Satan say – if I remember correctly – "Not to know me/Argues yourself unknown." '

'I've never believed I have the ability to become "known", and I've never wished I had it,' Maurice said in self-defence.

'Of course that's true, Maurice,' Finn said, 'and I am sorry to have been so stupidly provocative. I've even forgotten to tell you the main thing about Dawlish - that he is a writer. And now we are already within a few hundred yards of his house, and there are two other things you'd probably better know before you meet him: he is a widower and he has acquired a woman companion named Isolda.'

•

It was Isolda who opened the plain white front door to them after Finn had pressed the bell beside it. Smiling hospitably she turned from them for a moment and called out, 'Here's Jason Johnson and a friend.' So "Finn" had been only a nickname, borrowed no doubt from Mark Twain's Huckleberry Finn, Maurice guessed, as Frederick Dawlish appeared from a room farther back in the house and came forward to meet them.

An elderly man, plentifully grey-haired, looking younger than he almost certainly must be, Maurice thought, but in stature he was rather short, shorter perhaps than he had once been. His smile, when Jason introduced him to Maurice, was strangely gentleman-like. Then mock-severely he rounded on Jason, and asked, 'What's kept you away from me for so long?'

'My duties as Marshal,' Jason said.

'Yes,' Frederick said seriously. 'I do understand that you have to be more alert than ever to the threat from the outside world now.'

He turned to Isolda. 'What would you say to our having coffee in the front room?' he asked her.

'I'll get it,' Jason said. He was evidently on close enough terms with the Dawlish couple to know his way about in their kitchen.

He brought four cups of coffee on a tray into the front room, and Frederick and Isolda hurriedly extricated three small tables, with brown plastic tops grained to imitate wood, which were stacked under the arched front of a badly damaged genuine Sheraton sideboard. Isolda and Frederick hospitably shared one of the tables, the biggest, while Jason and Maurice each had a smaller one. And no coffee was spilt at all.

•

Suddenly Frederick said, 'Yesterday from this window I saw an amazing thing – a more brilliant and more extensive rainbow than I can remember ever having seen before, and then gradually around it at some distance from its outer rim a still more extensive one came clearly into view, though its colours were rather fainter. And the two of them seemed to remain like this for so long that I could almost have believed they might never disappear.'

Frederick had probably called Isolda to see these rainbows too, Maurice (who hadn't seen them) thought. But she did not say anything, nor did Jason, nor did Maurice.

•

At last Frederick spoke again.

'How beautiful, how beautiful,' he said, 'but the rainbows don't belong to this Garden City. They are part of the outside world, and we are deluding ourselves if we hope to exclude that world from here. In spite of Jason Johnson's truly heroic struggle, that world with its multiplying wars and its racist exterminations and its poisoning of the air and the seas for centuries to come – that world is what you are going to wake to, Maurice. And look, already you can see straight ahead of you the railway station you left two hours ago, and the signal is at green, and you are going to catch the train which will enable you to be in time to meet the school governors who will offer you the better job you wanted. And the influence this job will give you will help you to rally resistance among the people to the reactionaries, who if unopposed would bring about the horrors I have warned you of in your dream.'

•

'Do not despise dreaming, Maurice. In the battle you must face you will be strengthened by an awake dream of a future in which the whole human world has become one United Garden City.'

~ THE SUSPECT ~

ALL THE OTHERS in the dormitory seemed to remain asleep when Edgar was woken by a burly-bodied dark-suited man who stood close to his bed and prodded his shoulder with a thick finger.

'What's happened?', Edgar asked, still drowsy but alarmed.

'We are arresting you on a charge of incitement to acts of violence,' the man said.

Edgar was now aware of a second and very similar-looking man standing behind the first.

'What utter rubbish,' Edgar said.

'You can say what you like,' the first said, picking up from beside Edgar's bed a capacious black plastic bag which contained all his possessions, 'but for your own good you had better come quietly with us at once.'

Giving him no chance to answer or resist they seized him by his upper arms and after lifting him out of his bed they took him to relieve his bladder in the doorless latrine provided here, and when he'd finished they frog-marched him towards the stairs that led down from the dormitory to the street below. But they halted short of the stairs, and they made him stand up straight. Then the second man produced what appeared to be a child's paint brush which he dipped into a small tin of a liquid that looked like transparent varnish, and while the first man held Edgar's head rigidly moveless he quickly painted two thin vertical lines downwards over Edgar's eyes and on to his cheeks.

'You are blinding me,' Edgar said, trying to sound aggressively accusing in order to hide the fear he felt.

'No, I am not,' the painter said. 'The automatic reflex of your eyelids has kept the varnish from contacting your eyes.' He spoke the words 'automatic reflex' in a mechanical monotone which suggested that without clearly understanding them he had learnt them while attending a brief course on psychology for selected policemen, but they gave Edgar some slight reassurance. 'I am not blinding you,' the painter went on. 'Your face is dirty now, and the way I am using this varnish will ensure that thin lines of the dirt will be permanently preserved above and below your eyes. You will be indelibly marked for the rest of your life.'

The first man, evidently deciding that this talk had gone on long enough, flung an arm round Edgar's neck, and tightening his grip until Edgar was almost choking, he hauled him down the stairs and out to the pavement below.

There waiting at the kerb was a police car. The second man walked to the far side of this and got into a back seat. The first man shoved Edgar into the car beside the second, then got in himself, and Edgar was sandwiched painfully between them.

The drive lasted possibly five minutes – though to Edgar crushed between these two kidnapping plain-clothes policemen (or detectives, as he supposed them to be officially called) it seemed to last much longer. Eventually the driver brought his car to a stop outside a large solidly built redbrick police station, and the detectives pushed and pulled Edgar out of the car. A few of the people who had been walking along the pavement paused to watch with brief interest the two dark-suited men tightly gripping Edgar's arms and hurrying him into the station.

The Police-Sergeant inside the station undid the short piece of rope that was knotted round the top of Edgar's black plastic bag, and he poured its contents on to the surface of the desk at which he sat. Next he took a sheet of paper from one of the drawers of his desk and made a careful list of all the items that had been in the bag. These included Edgar's leather wallet from which the Sergeant drew out, and counted twice over, fifteen twenty-pound notes (to the astonishment of Edgar who couldn't remember ever having put more than two or three into the wallet), and he held each of them up to the light as if hoping to detect forgeries among them, but apparently he couldn't.

When he'd finished writing he passed pen and paper to Edgar and asked him to sign his name at the bottom of the list as a confirmation that he found it correct. Edgar was not unaware that a forged leaflet urging its readers to assassinate various members of the Government might have have been clandestinely slipped in among his other belongings by the Sergeant, but he decided he would do himself less harm by signing the list than by refusing to sign it.

Crooking a blue-sleeved arm the Sergeant swept all the contents of the bag off the surface of the desk and back into the bag, which he then carried to a khaki-coloured steel filing-cabinet in a corner of the room. He detached a bunch of keys from his belt, unlocked one of the steel drawers, dropped the bag into it, closed and relocked the drawer, and finally turning to the two detectives, who were still gripping Edgar's arms, he handed them another key, and said, 'This is the one you'll need.'

Edgar, who had been half-hypnotically watching every detail of the Sergeant's movements, was unpleasantly startled when he was jerked forward by the two detectives who held him.

The first of them unlocked a cell door and the second of them gave him an agonising thumb-jab in the kidneys before knocking him down and causing his head to hit the bare stinking floor of the cell extremely hard. Then not long afterwards the first detective reopened the cell door and threw a dirty mattress towards him, saying, 'You will be fed later.'

Edgar did not sleep much that night. His head ached continually. He was surprised next morning when a young policeman he hadn't seen previously – an assistant presumably to the Sergeant at the station – brought him quite a generous breakfast consisting of porridge and bacon and eggs and sausages and fried bread; also he was given plenty of coffee to drink – in a large white enamelled metal mug with a rim from which the enamel had been chipped off in several places.

'We are allowing you to go free today,' the young policeman said, and added surlily: 'We haven't sufficient evidence to support a charge of incitement to acts of violence.' Next, no doubt echoing what he'd heard his superiors say, he told Edgar menacingly: 'But we'll get you in the end.'

The Sergeant restored Edgar's black plastic bag to him and, after giving him time to urinate and defecate in the malodorous toilet here, led him to the outer door of the police station, saying expressionlessly as he opened it for him, 'You can go home now.'

Edgar walking freely along the pavement felt in spite of his headache an elation which survived for quite a while, until a sudden disturbing question came into his mind.

'Where is my home?'

Certainly it was not in that dreadful place he'd been taken from yesterday morning to a police cell which had seemed to him to have a noticeably similar urinary-faecal malodour. Perhaps his home was in a doorway, the kind of night refuge that a number of destitute but perfectly sane men preferred to the dosshouse accommodation the Government angrily blamed them for not availing themselves of. (Homeless women of course could find lodgings from which they were able to operate as prostitutes.) But Edgar knew he would not like sleeping in doorways. Was there no home for him anywhere? Hadn't there been a home for him when he'd been a child?

As soon as this thought came to him he decided to travel to the town he'd been born in. Having no idea where to find the main railway station of the seemingly big city he was in at present, he civilly questioned an inoffensive-looking stranger, who gave every sign of being genuinely pleased to be able to tell him how to get there. Also at the station itself he had the impression that, regardless of the capacious plastic bag he carried on his back, and of the thin black line indelibly painted down the lower part of his forehead and the upper part of his cheeks, neither the man at the window of the ticket office who sold him a ticket to his home town, nor anyone else around in the station, looked at him askance.

(He wondered whether a black man carrying a capacious plastic bag and having a thin white line painted down the lower part of his forehead and the upper part of his cheeks would have been as unsuspiciously looked at as he had been.)

•

There were no steam engines visible in the glass-roofed terminus where the train to his home town waited at platform number six which, he now remembered, it had always departed from in his boyhood.

He was glad the diesel-electric train he got into an end carriage of was a fast one. He had not forgotten the serious accident, killing many passengers, that had happened in his boyhood to the semi-fast train which used to change over from the slow to the fast line just about half-way between the terminus and his home station.

Owing to a signalling error on the fatal day, an express emerging from a tunnel had crashed into the middle (not the end) carriages of the train that was crossing over from the slower to the fast line, and besides killing so many of the passengers in this train it had also killed its own driver and some of the passengers in its own front carriages. He himself, now about to travel by the fast train because it was the one that happened to be at platform six when he arrived there, chose half-superstitiously the third carriage from the end to sit in. (The actual end carriage was the Guard's van and the carriage next to this was full of luggage and packages of various kinds.)

A brief incident during the journey made his heart thump with fright. At the very moment when his train was approaching the place where long-ago the express had crashed into the train that had begun to cross over from the slow to the fast line, he thought he saw the same thing about to happen again. But now what came suddenly out of a tunnel was a slow-moving locomotive trailing trucks behind it along a line which ran parallel with the fast line. Nevertheless the shock of the illusion persisted in Edgar long enough to make him fail, when the train stopped at his home station, to notice for a moment or two that he'd arrived there.

As he stepped out on to the platform he realised that he had left his large plastic bag behind in the luggage-rack of the compartment where he had been sitting, and he was only just in time to retrieve it before the train started to move again.

He was able with relief to hand in his ticket to the ticket-collector and to walk down out of the station into his home town. But his confidence about being able to find the house where he'd lived as a boy had been shaken by the mistakes he'd already made during his journey today. Now a large building obstructed the entrance to the street which he had expected to walk along towards the house, and he was beginning to wonder whether he might even find the street itself built over if he managed to circumvent the obstruction. And also the main street he was walking along in actuality seemed to come to an end a few hundred yards ahead of him. Then, just as he was beginning to feel totally lost, he reached an unobstructed side street which he at once recognised. Very clearly printed in black letters on a white background edged all round with a thin black line, the name Arthur

Road was displayed by an oblong metal street-sign affixed to a wall. He was sure Arthur Road led to the house he was so eager to see.

But that house, his boyhood home, was no longer to be seen. It had been replaced, he discovered, by a large block of flats; though strangely this block seemed to show an affinity architecturally with what it had supplanted. Perhaps its architect intended to pay apologetic homage to the dead architect whose house he had helped an entrepreneurial builder to destroy.

Edgar felt a pang of homesickness as he remembered the games he and his younger brother, Vernie, used to play with lead soldiers and clockwork railway engines on the nursery floor there, but he also remembered having unkindly excluded his brother Vaughan, who was a year and a half younger than Vernie, from taking part in these games (because he thought Vaughan was still too childish to be capable of playing them properly).

Vaughan, resenting his exclusion, had been able, however, to write a retaliatory poem about his older brothers:

Edgar and Vernie were kids of two
Their heads were made of glue
And when they hopped they genery dropped
They had a little topt
They hopt and the topt did dropt.

After reaching the age of eighteen Vaughan became ill with the disease then known as dementia praecox (and later less precisely as schizophrenia). He had to spend the rest of his life in mental hospitals, and Edgar was to remember this poem with sadness.

• • •

HE WALKED ON now, leaving the new flats behind him. He told himself that at least the public park he used to be so fond of was unlikely to have been sold by the Council, no matter how short of money they might be, to a 'developer'. He was confident that he would not find it converted into a Fair Ground with roundabouts and coconut shies.

The roadside path he walked along with his plastic bag slung over his shoulder led him soon to a very recognisable semi-humpbacked bridge, and he stopped to lean on the stone coping of the left-hand wall of the bridge and to look down at the water below. It was all as it used to be. He knew that three-quarters of the arch under the bridge had been bricked up, leaving only a narrow space for the local river to flow through, and the bricks held back enough water to form the artificial lake which he could see was here still, and most probably it still stretched far into the park just as it had done when he'd been a child.

Certainly the large wrought iron gates at the park entrance with their decorative curls and curves looked the same as ever, and so did the similarly decorative smaller gate now open beside them. But as he started going along the path by the lake, he saw on the far side of it rows of houses in place of the spacious green fields that were formerly there.

He felt disappointed, yet he did not allow his disappointment to weaken the belief he'd had, ever since being freed from the police station early today, that this town where he'd been born could be the home he longed to reach. The memory soon came to him of the kindergarten which he and Vernie had attended when he was nearly seven and Vernie was five. It was at Queensfield Lodge a little way farther along the road leading uphill from the park. He didn't for a moment expect to find it just as it had been in his childhood but he did let himself hope that the building still existed, or one similar to it and used for the same purpose of teaching very young children.

•

As he walked up the hill he remembered how much he had liked going to that kindergarten and how happy he had been with the other children there. And Mabel Durant, who taught them in her small sitting-room, was fond of them all and they liked her. She gave them biscuits and fruit-drinks at break-time and let them out, when the weather was fine, to play in the large garden of the Lodge; and on one unforgettable occasion they were allowed to eat all the ripe loganberries they could find there.

At Christmas, after she had given up the kindergarten and had got married, she sent them all a gilt-edged card across the back of which she had written:

Queensfield Lodge

Summer 1910

Wishing you a Merry Xmas & a Happy New Year

On the other side of the card she had very neatly pasted two admirably clear photographs of the kindergarten children, the lower one showing all five of them facing the camera: Edgar's brother Vernie on the left, then next to him Connie MacIvor and next to her Eileen Duncan, who was very pretty and was the cleverest of them all, and close beside her was Edgar with John Wheeler, rather a bumptious little boy, standing to the right of him at the end of the line. Each of the children was carrying a thin stick with a flag attached to it, and the flags were of various nations. (Evidently Mabel was no xenophobe.)

The children were carrying the same flags in the upper photograph too, though here Vernie was turning to speak to Eileen, entirely hiding Connie from the camera. Edgar later was to discover that Vernie had been just as much attracted by Eileen as he had. He was also to discover that at the local Girls' High school Connie had proved to be cleverer than Eileen – Connie herself had informed him of this before she had left the school. He hoped that the children who might be at a new kindergarten in Queensfield Lodge now would be less unlucky than most of those he had known at the old one.

He did not see Connie again after she had left school, but he was told by his mother that she had married a young solicitor and that within a few months of her marriage her solicitor husband had been found guilty of embezzlement and been sentenced to several years in prison. Eileen had become a doctor and, it was rumoured, had married a man who became unfaithful to her. And, unluckiest of all the kindergarten children, John Wheeler, who went to Osborne, the prep school for the Naval College at Dartmouth, died there after a mastoid operation. Dr Alston, Edgar's father, said that this was a disgrace. (And it happened that some while afterwards the authorities decided to shut the school down.)

Even now, so many years later, as he continued walking up the hill,

Edgar thought with fascination and admiration of Mabel. How could such a nice woman have been produced by such a family as the rest of the Durants were, female and male? He thought of her two sisters: Charlotte the middle one, so often pettish, who married a Master of Foxhounds in the West Country and was childless, and Lilian, the older one, an ever smiling never married church-worker who rode a bicycle with a back-pedal brake – like Miss Gee in Auden's heartless poem – and died of cancer; he thought also of the two Durant brothers, prim Colin, and joking Giles who was the youngest of the whole family. Their robustly rubicund stockbroker father was reported to have said of them at the golf-club: 'My son Colin? My son Colin is a rich man. My son Giles? My son Giles is a fool.' And what could Edgar remember about the Durant mother? He only once saw her. She had an anxious and ailing look, and she seemed to spend most of her time behind a large dark red screen in her drawing-room.

'Now they are all dead,' Edgar said to himself. Then suddenly the thought came to him that one of Mabel's children might be a living adult running a new kindergarten in the old building which he could now see ahead of him undestroyed.

•

As he neared it he became able to read, in white lettering on a blue enamelled metal plaque above the front door, the words:

QUEENSFIELD LODGE
A Registered Care Residence

How could he continue now to deceive himself with the hope that this town he was born in could be the home he'd set out from the police station to find?

And yet what was wrong with a town which allowed provision to be made for at least some people, no doubt mostly elderly, who could no longer care for themselves? And the fact that this residence was 'registered' ought to guarantee that the worst abuses would not occur there. (It was true that appalling instances of child abuse and cruel neglect of the elderly in registered, as well as unregistered, care residences had been exposed in other towns. However, these were comparatively rare and had been adequately sensationalised by the popular press.)

Edgar seemed to remember that William Blake had somewhere condemned devoted supporters of the struggle to liberate humanity in general who did little or nothing to relieve the sufferings of human beings in particular. Wasn't Edgar deserving of condemnation for deciding that a town which had converted a former kindergarten into a care residence could not be the home he had been trying to find?

Then he recognised that, without the devoted struggle for the liberation of the human race, the relief of particular victims would be constantly thwarted and would achieve little, and it might even be welcomed by the enemies of human liberation as a distraction from the struggle.

At last he became sure that there could be no home for him except in that struggle. And already he had a clear idea of where he could go to take part in it.

•

But now all at once he felt a violently sharp pain in his bowels. Something he'd been given to eat for breakfast at the police station must have disagreed with him, poisoned him perhaps. He picked up his black plastic bag and walked back hurriedly into the town to look for a public convenience.

Having found one, and having relieved himself, he went to wash his hands in the basin outside the closet, and looking up into the mirror above the basin he saw with momentary surprise that there was no black line above or below his eyes. The detective who had told him that he would be marked for life had been fooling him. The varnish was of an impermanent kind, and now its disappearance revealed that the lines of skin it had covered on Edgar's forehead were no dirtier than the skin of the rest of his forehead was. He gave his face a good wash before walking out into the street again.

He soon realised as he walked that he would be too late to catch a train now to the place where he believed he would find his real home. He would have to stay the night somewhere here in this town that had shown itself to be no longer the home-town it had once been for him.

But first he went to look for a shop which in his boyhood had sold leather goods of many kinds, and finding the shop still existed he bought a suitcase there, rather heavy, though with wheels fixed to one of its lower corners, and into it he packed the plastic bag containing all his possessions. He thought the suitcase would make him appear less like a penniless tramp when he asked for bed and breakfast at the only hotel of any sort he could remember in this town. He believed it had been called 'The White Hart', but on approaching its entrance he saw that it had a very different name at present – 'The Flask and Dildo'. The would-be clever but crude anachronistic humour of this name annoyed Edgar; nevertheless he entered the hotel and booked a room for the night.

Next morning after a substantial breakfast – he didn't eat it all – which was very similar to the one brought to him the previous morning by the young policeman, he walked wheeling his suitcase beside him to the railway station.

He took a slow train that according to the indication board would stop at every station on its way to the terminus. He wasn't sure which station he would have to get out at in order to find the building he hadn't seen for many years and was so keen to see again. He recognised nothing familiar among the mostly dismal-looking groups of terrace houses visible on the journey between the stations that the train stopped at, but he got out at the final stop before the line led on, as he remembered, under a series of smoky bridges and semi-tunnels to the terminus.

•

Now he did know where he was, and he knew the way to the building he wanted to see again. It had formerly been a Corn-Exchange, and the Town Council had gained possession of it and for a reasonable charge had allowed various organisations, regardless of their politics, to use it.

He did not have to walk far before reaching this building. Though shabbier on the outside than formerly, and needing a re-paint, it hadn't been bulldozed to the ground. It was undestroyed; and the door of the main entrance under a pillared canopy was open, with two broad-shouldered men standing outside it. A left-wing meeting could be taking place inside.

•

A vivid remembrance came suddenly to Edgar of his first attendance at a meeting in this building. He'd arrived late, having had some difficulty in finding it. When he entered it a young woman was making a speech from the platform, vehemently stating the urgent need for a second front on the continent to be started by Britain in support of the Soviet Union, which was already engaging the major section of the invading Nazi forces. This was an opinion he strongly held but had never expressed publicly. Hearing her speak had a lasting effect on him. He was soon aware that she and most of the other speakers were communists, and by the end of this meeting Edgar knew that he must do all he could to become worthy of being accepted eventually as a member of the Party.

Now, a few years after this (he couldn't have said precisely how many) he approached the two men guarding the entrance of the same though shabbier building.

'Welcome to you, comrade Alston,' one of the men said to him with a friendlily ironic emphasis on the word "comrade". Edgar recognised him as Willy Hardwick, whose meaning became clear when he went on to explain that among the men and women attending the meeting few if any used this word at present, possibly because it had been habitual among members of the Communist Party of Great Britain, which a number of them had belonged to before the dissolution of the Soviet Union. They preferred to use first names, whether these were their real first names or not. 'But there is one thing you'll find we are all agreed on,' Hardwick added, '– that there has been a revival of fascism in a new form and that we urgently need to create a new organisation to oppose and totally crush it.'

Soon after the meeting began there was a strange rumbling under the floor which grew louder and louder till the whole building shook and was finally lifted up high in the air as by a huge earthquake.

Next morning he woke, it seemed, from a long deep sleep and found himself on a mattress of what at first appeared to be a cell. There was someone standing beside him, a young man wearing a black uniform, who said to him, 'So you've woken up at last.'

Edgar looked dazedly around him and got the impression now that he was not in an ordinary police cell but in some kind of underground dugout.

'Where am I?' he asked.

'You were accidentally knocked unconscious among a dense crowd of shouting strike supporters,' the black-uniformed young man said, 'and I and some of my friends managed to rescue you before your neo-communist comrades could.'

'Who are you?'

'They call us neo-fascists, but we prefer to call ourselves Nationalists,' the young man said. 'We are holding you here until we decide what to do with you.'

'How long have I been unconscious?'

'Three days.'

'Will you please untie my hands and feet?'

'Certainly not. I have had enough trouble with you at nights even though I know you can't escape. You've given me hardly any rest with your noisy talking in your sleep, if your unconsciousness can be called sleep. You must have been having some weird dreams '

'How were they weird?'

'They sounded as if you believed you were still living in the twentieth century.'

'What do you mean?'

'It seems you haven't woken up sufficiently yet to know that you've lived through into the first year of the twenty-first century, and that there's a full-scale fourth World War on.'

Edgar could say nothing. He was now completely awake and realised that the fascist had not been lying to him. Horror came upon him, both because of the War and because of his own age, ninety-eight, which would make him of little use to the cause he had so long lived for.

•

There was a sudden sound of pickaxes crashing down on the roof of the dugout.

The black-uniformed young fascist had time to say to Edgar, 'Your neo-communist comrades may have won this battle here, and they will kill me when they break through into this dugout. But you will not live to be glad of their success.

•

He drew out a machine-pistol from a holster attached to his belt and shot Edgar in the face.